A Gift for the Children

A Gift
for the
Children

Pearl S. Buck

Illustrations by Elaine Scull

THE JOHN DAY COMPANY
New York
An Intext Publisher

The John Day Company, 257 Park Avenue South, New York, N.Y. 10010

Published on the same day in Canada by Longman Canada Limited.

Printed in the United States of America.

Library of Congress Cataloging in Publication Data

Buck, Pearl (Sydenstricker) 1892–1973.
    A gift for the children.

    SUMMARY: Twenty-one stories recount the adventures of children at Christmas and other times of the year.
    [1. Short stories. 2. Christmas stories]
I. Scull, Elaine, illus. II. Title.
PZ7.B879Gi   813'.5'2 [Fic]   73–7401
ISBN 0–381–99634–4

Contents

A Gift
for the
Children

A Note from the Publisher

Shortly before she died, Pearl Buck and I discussed the form this collection should take. As anyone who has loved her books knows, she approached all her writing with a fine and precise awareness of her reader. This book, however, presented somewhat of a problem, for it was directed to two audiences: First, the grandparent or parent who would acquire it as a gift for a child and who would, in many cases, read the stories aloud. Second, the youngster, who would come to these tales without knowing either the grand lady who wrote them or her very special place in the heart of the giver. Just how well the problem has been solved, I leave to you. We selected stories from across the entire sweep of her work, stories written for children of every age and, not surprisingly, written to warm the hearts of older readers as well. Because Christmas is such a special time for children, two of Miss Buck's famous Christmas stories are included.

A GIFT FOR THE CHILDREN is a "remembrance" book in the truest sense of the term. It is a part of our past, and hers. It gives the reader a rare opportunity to recall that past and to convey to the young its warmth and beauty. Finally, it is—so fittingly—Pearl Buck's own gift to the children, lovingly crafted during her last year, by which she, too, will be remembered.

Theodore B. Dolmatch
President
Intext Publishers Group

PART ONE

Stories for Little Children

Five Children

This is the house on the hill.

These are the five children who live in the house with their father and their mother.

Michael is the biggest. He has gray eyes and straight light hair. Michael likes green. He likes to wear a green suit. He likes to eat chocolate ice cream. He likes to play with his truck and his cars. He likes to hitch his cars together.

But he HATES TO PICK UP HIS TOYS.

Peter is next. He has brown eyes and brown hair. Peter likes red. He likes to wear red suits and eat red apples. He likes flowers and the moon and stars. He likes to watch beetles and little goldfish and tiny birds, and to find pretty pebbles.

But he HATES BIG NOISES.

David is next. He has dark blue eyes and curly brown hair. He likes dark blue. He likes to wear a dark blue suit with a white collar. He likes milk. He likes stories. Whenever his father or his mother sits down he runs for a book and says, "Please read me a story."

But he HATES TO GO TO BED.

Barbara and Judy are next, and they are twins.

Barbara has brown eyes and light hair. She likes pink and she likes to wear her pink coat and hat. She likes to eat eggs. She likes to sweep the floor, and put things away. She likes to clean and to wash.

But she HATES TO DRINK MILK.

Judy has blue eyes and brown curls. She likes pale blue, and she likes to wear her blue coat and hat. She likes to eat apples with Peter. She likes to sing and she likes to hear music. She likes to play with her dolls.

But she HATES TO RUN FAST.

Now you know the five children.

When Fun Begins

The children's house is not on the top of the hill and it is not at the bottom. It is halfway up the hill, so that when the children go down they come to the lake, and when they go up they come to a big tree.

One day the children came out to play.

"Let's go up the hill to the big tree," said Judy.

"No, let's go down the hill to the lake," said David.

"No—no," said Judy.

"Yes—yes," said David.

And everybody waited and nobody could go anywhere because they could not agree.

When all the five children want to do the same thing, then that means they agree. Sometimes they can agree, and sometimes they want to do different things and they cannot agree.

Then Daddy came out to play, too.

"Where are we going?" he asked the children.

"Up the hill to the big tree," said Judy.

"Down the hill to the lake," said David.

"We can't go anywhere unless we agree," said Daddy.

So he sat down on the porch and waited. They all sat and waited. And nobody had any fun.

Then Michael thought of something.

"Let's climb up the hill to the tree and then run fast down the hill to the lake," he said.

"That's a good idea," said Daddy, and he asked Judy, "Do you agree?"

"Yes," said Judy.

"David, do you agree?" asked Daddy.

"Yes," said David.

"Does everybody agree?" asked Daddy.

"Yes!" all the children shouted together.

So they all climbed up the hill to the big tree and it was fun.

Then they ran down the hill to the lake. On the lake was the rowboat, and the children got in. Three of the children sat at the back and they were the boys. Two of the children sat in front and they were the girls. In the middle sat Daddy and he rowed the boat. If he rowed up the lake they would go to the woods. If he rowed down the lake they would come to the falls.

"Which way shall we go?" asked Daddy.

"Up the lake," said the girls.

"Down the lake," said the boys.

"If I do both at the same time," said Daddy, "we'll just go round and round. Which way shall I go first?"

"Up!" said the girls.

"Down!" said the boys.

And again they could not agree and so Daddy

rowed the boat round and round in a circle and they went nowhere at all and nobody had any fun.

"But we want to go to the woods," said Barbara.

"We want to go to the falls," said Michael.

"You'll have to agree," said Daddy, and he just kept going round and round.

The girls looked at the boys and the boys looked at the girls. And Daddy waited and waited and the boat kept going round and round while they waited and still nobody had any fun. Then Peter thought of something.

"Let's let the wind tell us which way to go first," he said.

"That's a good idea," said Judy.

"Do you agree?" Daddy asked the girls.

"Yes!" they said.

"Do you agree?" Daddy asked the boys.

"Yes!" they said.

"Then look at the clouds," Daddy said, "and see which way the wind blows."

They all looked up at the sky. It was blue and there were little soft white clouds hurrying across it, and they were all hurrying up the lake to the woods.

"What does the wind say?" Daddy asked.

"It says, to the woods," Barbara said.

"To the woods," they all agreed.

"Now we can begin our fun," Daddy said. "First we will go to the woods and then we will go to the falls."

And so they did, and it was fun.

Thunder

One day it was very hot. The children and their mother had taken their lunch to the lake and all day long they played in the water and under the trees. They were so busy having a good time that they did not look at the sky. Suddenly they heard a big noise.

"What's that?" Michael asked.

"That is thunder," Mother said. They looked at the sky. It was bright blue over their heads but beyond the house were big clouds like dark mountains with silvery-white edges.

"Those are thunder clouds," Mother said, "and they will bring us rain."

"I don't like thunder," Judy said, and she wanted to cry, but she didn't.

"Thunder can't hurt you," Mother said, "it's just a big noise."

"I don't like such a big noise," Peter said.

"I like a big truck noise, but I don't like this thunder noise," said Michael.

Just then there was a quick bright light.

"What's that?" asked David.

"That is lightning," Mother said. "Listen a minute and you will hear thunder."

They listened and sure enough, in a minute they heard thunder, and this time it was louder than before.

"It makes me afraid!" Judy said, and now she began to cry a little.

Mother took her hand. "We will go home," Mother said, "because thunder and lightning usually bring rain. Rain is good for flowers and grass and trees, but children go inside the house until it is over."

"What is lightning?" asked Michael, who likes to ask "what" questions.

"Lightning is electricity in the clouds," Mother said. "It makes a light there just as it does in our home when you put on the lights at night. But in the clouds the light cuts the clouds like a big bright knife. Then the clouds clap together again and what we hear is the clap and we call it thunder."

"Why does lightning cut the clouds?" Michael asked, because he likes to ask "why" questions.

"That is just the way it is," Mother said, "and we don't know why. Let's hurry, for here comes the rain."

The rain was coming down fast.

"How does the rain come?" asked Michael, who likes to ask "how" questions.

"The clouds get so heavy they can't hold the rain any more and so they let it down," said Mother. "Hurry, hurry, or we'll be wet!"

And then they heard Daddy calling, "It's a big rain. Hurry, hurry, or you'll all be wet!" and he hurried to meet them and they all took hands and ran home out of the rain.

But the trees and grass and flowers, of course, stayed just where they were and they liked the rain, for it washed them clean and gave them fresh water to drink.

The Sun

The five children were eating supper. While they were eating their junket Peter saw something on the floor.

"Oh, look!" he cried.

They all looked and they all saw something on the floor, too. It was long and bright and shining.

"I will pick it up and see what it is," said David.

"Try," said Mother.

So David got down from his chair and tried to pick it up. But he could not do it.

"I will sweep it up for you," said Barbara.

"Try," said Mother.

So Barbara went out to the kitchen and found the broom and brought it into the dining room and she swept as hard as she could, but she could not sweep it up. It was still on the floor.

"What is it?" asked Michael.

"Is it a white rope?" Mother asked them.

"No!" they all shouted.

"Is it a silver ribbon?" asked Mother.

"No!" they all shouted.

"Is it bright water?" asked Mother.

"No!" they all shouted.

"Is it shining paper?" asked Mother.

"No!" they all shouted.

"Is it a sunbeam?" asked Mother.

"Yes!" they all shouted.

And a sunbeam is what it was and that is why David could not pick it up in his hand, and Barbara could not sweep it up with her broom.

"Where does it come from?" Michael asked.

"Let's follow it and see," said Mother.

Their junket was finished by this time, so they got down and walked in the sunbeam and walked right up to a window.

"Look out of the window, and up the hill," Mother told them.

They looked, and there was the sun, just going down behind the hill.

"The sunbeam came from the sun," said Mother. "Now watch to see what happens."

So they watched, and while they watched the red sun went down behind the hill.

"Oh, where's the sunbeam?" Peter cried.

They all turned around to find it, but it was gone.

"The sun took it with him," Mother said.

"Where is the sun going?" David asked.

"He's going over the hill and down the sky to the other side of the world," Mother said.

"What will the sun do on the other side of the world?" Michael asked.

"He will give light and sunbeams to other children," Mother said.

"Why?" asked Michael.

"Because there is only one sun for everybody," Mother told him, "and so we all take turns with it. While you sleep it is night and the sun gives light for the children on the other side of the world so they can play. It is their turn. Then in the morning the sun comes back to you, and it is your turn to play and that is how the sun makes day and night for everybody."

"Will the sun be sure to come back tomorrow?" David asked.

"I don't want those other children to keep my sun, maybe," Judy said.

"The sun comes back every morning," Mother said. "No one can keep the sun. If there are no clouds in the sky we will see it again tomorrow when you wake up."

The Clouds

The next morning when Mother went into the children's rooms the children were waking up.

"Did the sun come back?" David asked.

"Let's go to the window and see," Mother said. "Look over the lake."

So the children climbed out of their beds and ran to the window.

"But we saw the sun last night behind the hill," Michael said, "so why do we look over the lake this morning?"

"The sun went down in the west, and that is behind the hill," Mother said.

"The sun had been all around the earth while you slept, and now it is coming up on the other side over the lake, and that is east," Mother said.

They all looked over the lake where the east was. But there was no sun. The sky was gray.

"Where is the sun?" Peter cried.

"It didn't come back," said David.

"Yes, it is there," Mother said. "It is just behind the clouds. The light is shining through the clouds."

"I don't see the light," Michael said.

"What can you see?" Mother asked.

"I can see the lake," Michael said.

"And I can see a robin in the grass," Peter said.

"And I can see my red wagon I left outside last night," said David.

"And I can see the swing," Barbara said.

"I see smoke coming out of the chimney," Judy said.

"And I see all of you," Mother said smiling. "We all see, and that's because there is light, and there is light because the sun has come back and is there, shining behind the clouds. We will wait until the clouds go away, and then we will see the sun, too. Maybe it will send the sunbeam again."

All morning the children played and had a good time together, and then suddenly when they were riding their red wagons down the hill, something bright was upon the grass.

"The sunbeam!" Peter cried.

And it was the sunbeam. The clouds had moved a little and the sunbeam was shining down from the sun behind the clouds.

The Rainbow

The five children were playing in the sandpile under the maple tree. They were making tunnels and wells and houses and roads in the
sand. They were playing so hard that nobody had
time to look up or to look around. Suddenly they
heard patter—patter—patter, and drop—drop—drop.
Then they all looked up. It was rain. While they were
playing a big black cloud had slipped up from behind the hill and when it was over their heads it let
down its rain.

"Oh go away, rain!" Barbara cried.

"No, let the rain fill my well," David said.

"I don't want the rain to spoil my road," said Michael.

But the rain went on, no matter what they said, and
they all ran for the porch.

"I don't like rain," Judy said and looked cross.

"I don't like it, either," Michael said. "It is too wet."

While they talked, the cloud moved on its way
across the sky, carrying the rain with it, and the sun

26

shone again, and it shone on the falling rain that the cloud was taking away, and the children saw something they had never seen before. It was like colored ribbons hanging in the sky.

"I see red!" Peter said. Peter likes red.

"I see green!" Michael said. Michael likes green.

"I see blue!" Judy said. Judy likes blue.

"I can't see my pink," Barbara said. "There isn't any pink!" Barbara likes pink.

"You may take yellow," David said, "and I will take orange."

Just then Mother came to the window.

"Children!" she called, "do you see the rainbow?"

"Yes—yes," they all called back.

"But we didn't know it was a rainbow," Peter said.

"Who put it there?" Michael asked.

"The sun caught the rain," Mother said, "and it makes each little drop shine like a bubble."

The cloud kept moving while they watched and it grew smaller and smaller and the rainbow faded away. Soon there was only the sun shining on the wet grass and the children went back to their play.

But Peter always sees small pretty things. And by the sandbox he saw a raindrop on the edge of a blade of grass.

"Look!" he said.

They all looked, and there in the drop was a little rainbow, like the one they had seen across the sky, but it was very, very little.

"That's a rainbow for my dollies," Judy said.

What the Children Do in Summer

This is what Michael likes to do in the summer.

Michael likes to put on his bathing suit and jump into the pool. He likes to go down—down—down— until the water is over his head. Then he pops up again and swims all around the pool. "I like to pop up," Michael says.

This is what Peter likes to do in summer.

Peter likes to go down to the brook and take off his shoes and stockings and wade in the water and look for bright stones. He finds red ones and green ones and brown ones and yellow ones. "They are pretty stones," Peter says, and he keeps them in a box.

This is what David likes to do in the summer.

David likes to find wild strawberries hiding in the grass. He picks them and eats them. "I like the strawberries," David says.

This is what Barbara likes to do in the summer.

Barbara likes to take off her shoes and stockings and run in the grass. The grass is cool and soft on her bare feet. She laughs and laughs. "The grass tickles my feet and makes me laugh," Barbara says.

This is what Judy likes to do in the summer.

Judy likes to walk on the hill and pick all the flowers she can find and put them in her doll house for the dolls. "The dolls like the flowers," she says.

The Star

Once upon a time the children were at the beach in the summer. Every day they played in the sea and every night they looked at the stars. There were plenty of stars at the beach, and they were the same stars that the children saw in the sky at home over their house on the hill.

But one night there was another star and Peter saw it. It was a special star. It was not over the hill and it was not over the beach, and this is the story of how Peter saw it.

The children were coming home from the beach. First they had to get on a boat, and then they had to get on a train to sleep. When they got off the boat it was already dark. There was a crowd of people and everybody was calling and talking and making a big noise. The train was making a big noise, too. It whistled and puffed out smoke and said, "Hurry—hurry —hurry—"

And everybody hurried.

Now Peter had hold of Mother's hand, so he was all right. But he could not see where he was going. All around him were big people and he could only see knees and feet, knees and feet.

Then he looked up at the sky.

"Oh!" he shouted in such a loud voice that people looked down at their feet to see where the voice came from. And his mother thought something must be the matter, so she looked down very quickly, too, and said,

"What is it, Peter?"

"I see a star!" he cried in the same loud clear voice.

He did see it, in the sky through the little hole up above him between the big people. And everybody stopped just a minute to look up, too, and they all saw the star, bright and beautiful above them, and for that minute they were quiet.

"That's my star," Peter said.

The Snow

It was nearly Christmas and Daddy said, "Now it is winter and soon there will be snow." It had been such a long time since last winter that some of the children could not remember snow.

"What color is it?" asked Judy.

"It is white," Mother said.

"Will it burn me?" Judy asked again.

"It's as cold as ice cream," Daddy said.

"Can we eat it?" David asked.

"It has no taste," Mother said.

"Can we play with it?" Barbara asked.

"Yes, you may," said Daddy, "and I am going to buy you some shovels and sleds all ready for the snow."

"Red ones, please," said Peter.

So Daddy bought red shovels and red sleds, and the children waited and waited. Every morning they looked out of the window but there was no snow.

"It comes out of the sky," said Mother, so the children looked at the sky, and there was no snow.

"It lies on the ground," said Daddy, so the children

looked at the ground, but still there was no snow, and they all grew tired of waiting.

Then one day when they got up from their beds they looked out of the window as they always did, and something was falling down from the sky and something was lying on the ground.

"Snow!" they all shouted.

It was snow, and as fast as they could they ate their breakfasts and put on their snowsuits and took their shovels and their sleds and went outside.

Everybody had to touch the snow and taste it.

"It is white," said Judy.

"It is cold," said Michael.

"It has no taste," said David.

"We can play with it," said Barbara.

And every one of the five children did something different in the snow.

"I'm going to dig in the snow with my red shovel," said Michael, and he did.

"I'm going to make a snowman," said Peter, and he did.

"I'm going to roll in the snow and make myself all white," said Barbara, and she did.

"I'm going to slide on my red sled," said Judy, and she did.

"And I'm going to make a big snow hill," said David, "and then I'm going to dig a hole in it and go inside," and he did.

And the five children each did what he liked to do, and they had five different kinds of fun in the snow.

Tracks
in the
Snow

When the snow first fell it lay smooth upon the ground. But one day when the children went out they saw some marks on the smooth snow.

"Oh, look!" said Peter.

They all looked. There were four little marks, two in front and two behind.

"What's that?" Michael asked his mother.

"Those are rabbit tracks," Mother said. "Let's follow them and see which way the rabbit went."

So they all walked together following the tracks. Up the hill the tracks went to the vegetable garden.

"That's because the rabbit was hungry and went to see if there were any cabbages left in the garden," said Mother.

The tracks went round and round and up and down the garden.

"He was hunting and he couldn't find any cabbage," said Mother.

The tracks went down to a little dogwood tree.

"He has been chewing the bark off the dogwood tree," Mother said.

The tracks went round and round the tree.

"The rabbit has chewed all around the tree," David said. They saw where the rabbit had chewed off the bark.

The tracks went to the rose garden.

"If he has chewed my roses, he is a naughty rabbit," Mother said.

They all went to the rose garden and looked at the roses behind the stone wall. The rabbit had chewed the stems of the rosebushes just above the snow.

"Oh, naughty rabbit!" said Judy.

"Let's go and find him," said David. "Let's tell him he mustn't eat the rosebushes."

So they followed the tracks down the hill and around a bush and under the end of a log they saw a hole. The tracks went down the hole.

"The hole is his house," said Mother. "We will wait for him to come out."

They brushed the snow from the log and sat down and waited. But no rabbit came out.

"Maybe he's not at home," Peter said.

"Shall I find a stick and poke into the hole?" David asked.

"No, indeed," Mother said, "I wouldn't like that if I were a rabbit, would you?"

"No—no," said David, "I wouldn't." So he didn't do it.

Then Barbara thought of something. She got up and put her face close to the hole and shouted in a big loud voice,

"Rabbit, you have company—come out!"

The rabbit heard her, and he jumped out in such a hurry that Barbara fell over backward. But the rabbit went hopping away and all they could see was his white tail bobbing behind him on the snow.

The children were so surprised that they forgot to tell him why they had come.

"Never mind," Mother said. "We'll have to excuse him this time for eating the rosebushes. It is hard for hungry rabbits to find their breakfast on such a snowy morning."

What Happens in Spring

Peter got up one morning at the end of winter. The sun came in at his window.

"I want to go to the woods to play today," he said.

"That is a good idea," Mother said. "We will all go."

After breakfast all the children put on their outside play suits and went to the woods. They had not been there for a week because every day it had rained. Something had happened in the woods while they were away. Lots of things had happened. This is what they found.

Peter said, "Oh, look!" He saw something on the ground and he stooped to see it better. Then everybody came to see it. "It's a flower!" Peter said. And it was, a tiny white flower.

"It is a spring beauty," Mother said.

"Oh, look!" Michael said. And Michael saw something soft and bright and fuzzy on a little tree.

"I know what that is—a pussy willow," Peter said. And it was a pussy willow.

"Oh, look!" Barbara said. She had found a little nest in a bush. It was not finished yet.

"Let's leave it," Mother said. "A little bird is going to make a house there this spring and lay some eggs."

"Oh, look!" said Judy. And everybody looked, and there was a green frog beside the bush, looking very sleepy.

"He has just waked up from his long winter nap," Mother said.

"Oh, look at what I see!" David said in a big voice.

They all looked and there on a log in the warm sunshine they saw a little gray snake lying very still.

"The snake has been asleep, too," Mother said. "But now it is spring, so he wakes up."

"Shall I throw a stone at him?" David asked.

"No, because this little snake doesn't hurt people," Mother said. "He has just come out as we have to find some sunshine."

All day the children played until night. Then they were tired and ready for bed. They had their baths. They put on their pajamas. They brushed their teeth. Daddy and Mother read them each a story, and then they tucked them in bed. Daddy opened the windows. Outside it was dark. But in the dark Peter heard a noise. It was like this: Peep—peep—peep!

It was a little noise, but the children all heard it.

"What's that? What's that?" they all asked.

"Peepers," said Daddy. "They are little frogs and they are down by the lake in the woods."

"Why do they sing at night?" Peter asked.

"So we will remember even at night that spring has come," Daddy said.

Peter and the Squirrel

Mother was planting pansies. Peter came outside.

"I have three peanuts in my pocket," Peter said, "and I'm going to the woods to give them to the squirrels."

"That will be nice," Mother said, and she went on planting pansies.

So Peter went to the woods all by himself with the three peanuts in his pocket. Down the hill he went and along the lake and then he came to the woods. But he could not see any squirrels.

"Squirrels, where are you?" he called.

But no squirrels came.

So he went on and on, all by himself, until he was nearly in the middle of the woods. Then he stopped and looked around but still he could not see any squirrels.

"Squirrels, I have three peanuts for you!" he called. But no squirrels came.

So he went on and on, and then he *was* in the

middle of the woods. It was very quiet. Nobody was there except Peter. He heard a little rustling noise. It was the wind playing in the trees. He heard a little tinkling noise. It was the water in the brook, playing around the stones. And that was all.

And then suddenly right in front of him there was a plop, and he looked and it was a gray squirrel that had jumped down out of a tree. It stood up on its hind legs and it looked at Peter with its bright black eyes.

Then Peter said, "Oh, here you are, Squirrel! I've brought you three peanuts."

He took a peanut out of his pocket and threw it to the squirrel, and the squirrel picked it up with his front paws and opened it and ate it. Then Peter gave the squirrel the second peanut, and he opened that one and ate it in the same way. Then Peter gave the squirrel the third peanut and he opened that one and ate it, too.

"That's the last peanut, Squirrel," Peter said. "I haven't any more," and he put his hand into his empty pocket to show the squirrel that all the nuts were gone.

But the squirrel could not understand what Peter said, and he thought Peter put his hand in his pocket to get another peanut and so he waited. When he grew tired of waiting, he gave a little hop toward Peter just to show him he would like more peanuts.

And what do you think? Peter didn't understand the squirrel, either! When the squirrel hopped toward Peter he turned around and ran for home, and the squirrel thought he was running away with the peanuts and so he hopped after him.

"Mother, Mother!" Peter shouted, "the squirrel is chasing me!"

And Mother, looking up from her pansies, saw Peter running up the hill as hard as he could and the squirrel hopping after him as hard as *he* could.

"It's a great big squirrel!" Peter shouted, and he ran faster and so the squirrel hopped faster.

"Oh, it's getting bigger and bigger!" Peter shouted, looking over his shoulder. And then he began to cry.

His mother hurried to him and caught him in her arms and said,

"Stop, Peter! Turn around and look."

As soon as his mother came, Peter stopped and turned around and there was the squirrel. The squirrel had stopped, too, and he stood on his hind legs and waited for more peanuts.

Mother laughed. "Is it a big squirrel?" she asked.

And Peter looked and looked and he was very much surprised.

"Why, it's only a tiny little squirrel," he said.

At Supper

It was raining hard, and the children had to stay indoors to play. The day was long and it grew longer and longer. The children were tired.

At last it was suppertime. They went to the table and they all began talking at once.

"I don't want my porridge," said Michael.

"I don't like junket," said Barbara.

"Do I have to eat my lettuce?" asked Judy.

"I won't eat my applesauce," said David.

They made so much noise that nobody could hear anybody. All that they could hear was a big noise.

But Peter heard something else.

"Hush!" he said. "Listen!"

He put up his hand and the other children forgot their noise and listened.

"I hear a music," Peter said.

They all heard it. It tinkled and splashed and it was not too loud and it was not too soft. They listened and every time somebody began to talk Peter put up his hand. "Hush!" he said. So they listened again.

"What is it?" Judy whispered.

"What is it?" Michael whispered.

"Rain music," Mother whispered, "rain on the roof."

"Hush!" Peter said.

So they hushed and they listened and they heard it, tinkle and splash, tinkle and splash, and before they knew it Michael had eaten his porridge and Barbara had eaten her junket, and Judy's lettuce was gone and so was David's applesauce.

As for Peter, he ate up everything while he listened to the rain on the roof.

The Moon

It was night. The sun was gone and the sky was dark. In the house the children had finished their supper. They had played and taken their baths. They had on their pajamas and were ready to go to bed.

Then Daddy said, "But first look out of the big window and see what is coming up over the hill."

"I want to see, too," said Mother.

Daddy, Mother, and the children went to the big window and looked out.

"I can't see anything," said David.

"Wait," said Daddy.

"I can't see anything, either," said Judy.

"Wait," said Mother.

So they all waited at the big window and they all watched the dark sky at the tip of the hill.

"I see something now," said Michael.

"I see a light," said Peter.

They all looked. It was a light. At first it was small,

but it grew bigger and bigger until it spread up into the dark sky.

"Something behind the hill is making the light," said Barbara.

"Something is coming up over the hill," said Judy.

It came up over the hill. It was round and big and yellow. It climbed up the sky over the trees. It hung in the sky and everybody saw it. It was the moon.

"Who put that moon up there?" asked David.

"Did a truck bring it?" asked Michael.

"No," said Daddy.

"No," said Mother.

"Maybe it came on a train," said Barbara.

"Maybe it came up out of a hole in the ground," said Judy.

"No," said Mother.

"No," said Daddy. "It is always in the sky."

"Can it come out?" said Michael.

"No," said Daddy. "It has to stay in the sky."

"But sometimes I can't see it," said Peter.

"That is because it has gone to somebody else's place," said Daddy.

And then Daddy told them, "The moon goes round and round the world and up and down the sky. When it comes to our place we can see it. All the people in all the places in the world can take turns in looking at the same moon."

The Dark

Ome day the children were playing outside with their trucks and their tricycles. They were having such fun they did not know what time it was. Then Mother came out on the porch. She saw that the sun was gone and the dark was coming. She called to the children,

"Children, put your trucks and tricycles away, please. It will soon be dark."

Michael began to grumble.

"I wish the night wouldn't come. I wish I could play all the time."

"I don't want to go to bed all the time every night!" David cried.

But Peter didn't say anything. He just looked around. He saw the sun was gone from the sky, and he saw the dark beginning under the trees. And there was no moon tonight. It was already so dark he could not see the lake at all. And then he hurried and put his tricycle in the barn and he ran across the lawn to the porch where Mother was waiting.

"Let's go in the house," he told Mother.

"Just a minute," Mother said. "We must wait for the other children."

Peter held Mother's hand while they waited. When the other children came they all went into the house and Peter turned on the light quickly. He turned on the light in the playroom and he turned on the light on the stairs. Everywhere he went he turned on the light.

When the children had all had their baths and their suppers, their stories and their good-night kisses, and were tucked in their beds, Daddy began to turn out the lights. First he turned out the lights in the girls' room.

"Good night, dears," he said.

"Good night, Daddy," they said.

Then Daddy turned off the light in Michael's and David's room.

"Good night, dears," he said.

"Good night, Daddy," they said.

And then Daddy went into Peter's room. Peter sleeps in a little room by himself. He was in bed, all covered up to his chin.

"Daddy, please don't turn out the light," Peter said in a very low little voice.

Daddy was surprised. "Why, Peter!" he said. "And why not turn out the light?"

"Because," Peter answered, "I don't want the dark to come into my room." And now his voice was so little that Daddy could scarcely hear it.

"Why, Peter," Daddy said, "are you afraid of the dark?"

"*Yes!*" said Peter in a whisper, and without any voice at all.

Daddy sat down and remembered as hard as he could.

"When I was a little boy," he remembered, "I was afraid of the dark, too."

"Are you now?" Peter asked.

"No," Daddy said. "I don't have to be afraid any more because now I know what the dark is."

"What is it?" Peter asked.

"It is just the sun gone away to let us rest," Daddy said. "If the sun didn't go away, it would be too bright for us to sleep and, if we never went to sleep, we would soon be too tired to work and play. And all the animals and the plants would be too tired to grow. So the sun goes away awhile every day and lets us all rest in the good dark."

"Is that all?" Peter asked.

"That's all," Daddy said. "Now shall I turn out the light?"

"Yes," Peter said. And he went to sleep in the good and quiet dark.

PART TWO

Stories for Older Children

The
Chinese
Story Teller

Susan and Ricky were two children who lived with their father and mother on a farm. They lived next door to their grandmother, who lived by herself. She was an old lady, but not too old. Still, she was old enough to have white hair and she did not like too much noise.

"When you go to see Grandmother," the children's mother said, "it would be nice if you did not run around and shout."

"What shall we do, then?" Ricky asked. He was five years old.

"Suppose you sit down on the carpet beside Grandmother's chair and ask her to tell you a story. Her head is full of stories," the mother said.

"Why is Grandmother's head full of stories?" Susan asked. Susan was six years old.

"Because," her mother said, "your grandmother is not like other grandmothers. She grew up in China."

"Where is China?" Ricky asked.

"On the other side of the world," his mother said.

"How did Grandmother come here?" Ricky asked.

"She came on a ship," his mother said, "and it took a whole month. Now of course it would take only two or three days, because we could take an airplane and quickly get across the great Pacific Ocean."

"Let's go and see Grandmother now," Susan said to Ricky.

Since it was a Saturday morning and their mother was busy cleaning the house, she thought this was a good idea. So in a few minutes Susan and Ricky walked across the meadow down the hill to the brook. On the way they picked a pretty bunch of daisies for their grandmother and at the brook they jumped from one stone to another so they would not get their feet wet as they crossed to the other side. Then there was a small hill to climb and so at last they were at Grandmother's house. It stood beside a big walnut tree. On warm summer days Grandmother liked to sit in a comfortable chair in the shade of the walnut tree, and this morning, as Susan and Ricky came to the top of the hill, they saw she was there under the tree, reading a book.

When Grandmother saw them coming she closed the book and put it on a small table beside the chair. Then she called to them in her cheerful voice.

"Good morning, my dears. I was hoping you would come to see me today."

"We brought you some flowers," Susan said.

Grandmother took the flowers. "Thank you," she said. "Daisies are my favorite flowers."

"Why?" Ricky asked.

"Because," Grandmother said, "when I was married, a long time ago, my bouquet was made of daisies and little pink roses. Susan, will you get a glass of water for me from the kitchen? I will put the daisies in the water before they wilt."

Susan ran away to the kitchen to get the glass of water and Ricky sat down on the grass by Grandmother's chair. Just at this moment Ricky's dog, Barky, came running up the hill. He had been out hunting rabbits when Susan and Ricky left home, but he saw them climbing the hill and he ran after them as fast as he could. His name was Barky because he barked so much. Even now, before he could catch his breath, he began barking.

Grandmother and Ricky turned their heads to see why he was barking. Susan was coming back with the glass of water in both hands, but of course he was not barking at Susan, because he knew her. Susan put the glass on the table. Grandmother put the flowers into it. Then they saw why Barky was barking. It was because Grandmother's cat, Tizzy, was following Susan. She had been asleep by the kitchen door, but she woke up when Susan came out, and thinking that perhaps there was milk in the glass, she decided to follow and see. She was called Tizzy because when she was a kitten she had liked to chase her own tail. She would go round and round until Grandmother would call out to her, "You'll chase yourself into a tizzy!" So Grandmother named her Tizzy.

When Barky saw Tizzy come closer he ran at her, barking very loudly. Tizzy was an old cat now and she decided she would not run away. After all, Grandmother's house was her house, too, and she did not like dogs. So she puffed out her tail, she hissed and spat, and when Barky came closer, dancing on all four feet, Tizzy suddenly put out her paw and scratched his nose. Barky howled with pain and stepped back.

"Tizzy!" Grandmother called. "Behave yourself! Barky is only a visitor here."

"Barky!" Ricky called. "Go home!"

Barky did not want to go home and he whined to say so. But Tizzy came closer and closer and he decided that perhaps Ricky was right and he had better go home. So he put his tail between his hind legs and trotted down the hill. As for Tizzy, she licked her paw clean, washed her face, and since the glass had no milk for her, she went back to the kitchen door to sleep in the sun.

"Why don't cats like dogs?" Susan asked Grandmother.

"And why don't dogs like cats?" Ricky asked.

"Well," Grandmother said, "I don't really know, and so I can only tell you what I heard, long ago when I was a little girl in China. I was six years old, like Susan, and I had a gray kitten. Then someone gave me a puppy, and cat and dog did not like each other. Oh yes, being small, they learned to get along with each other, but they were not really friends. And then one day I heard an old man, who was a story teller, telling a story about why cats and dogs seem never to like each other."

"Tell us, please, Grandmother," Susan said.

"What is a story teller?" Ricky asked.

"A man who tells stories, of course," Susan said. Since she was a year older than Ricky, she felt she knew more than he did.

"But I want Grandmother to tell me—not you! You're always telling me things."

Grandmother laughed. "Now don't you two begin to act like cat and dog," she said, "and I'll begin now, before you make a fight. I'll begin at the very beginning, with the Chinese themselves. Well, the Chinese are such an ancient people, they have lived so long in one place, and there are so many of them that they have a reason for everything. I am not sure that all the reasons are true—that I cannot promise you. I can only tell you what the reasons are, as the Chinese *say* they are.

"For example, the reason why dogs don't like cats! Well, so it is all over the world, but especially it was so in China. All dogs in China seem to chase a cat whenever they see one. When they even smell a cat they will chase the smell. That much *is* true.

"In China there are many story tellers and they tell their stories just anywhere, sometimes in a teashop, sometimes under a little tent, sometimes just standing by the roadside. People stop to listen and if they like the story they put a penny or two into the little basket which the story teller passes around. If you hurry away just before he passes that basket then it is considered shamefully mean and so no one does it except very mean people.

"I was taking a walk one day on the village street where we lived and I saw a little crowd of people—Chinese people, of course—who were listening to a story teller, so I stopped, too. The story teller was sitting on a bamboo stool in the middle of the crowd. He was

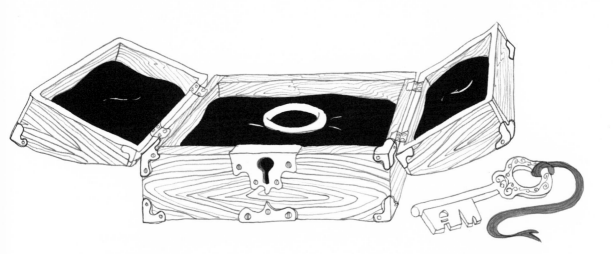

a small cheerful man, with a few whiskers on his face and a nice sing-song voice.

"Once upon a time," the story teller said, for a new story was just beginning, a story about why cats and dogs don't like each other. "There were a man and his wife who lived by a river. They were quite poor and they had to work very hard indeed. Their home was only a hut, with walls made of mud and the roof of straw. They had no children, for they were so poor that they feared they would not be able to feed them. Instead they kept a dog to watch the door when they had to go out to work, and a cat to catch the mice so they would not have their little bit of food eaten.

"One day when the man was coming home from work he felt something in the dust of the road. He was barefoot as usual, for he had no money to buy shoes, and he stooped and picked the thing up. It was a rusty old ring. He looked at it and he did not think it worth anything. Nevertheless, because he was so poor he kept it and when he got home he showed it to his wife. 'This is no treasure,' she said.

"But they never threw anything away and so they just put it into a drawer and forgot it. They worked as usual, were always hungry, and then a strange thing began to happen. Where before all had been unlucky for them, now everything began to be lucky.

"Their fields grew wonderful crops, their hens all laid eggs, they found fine fish in their pond, and they got high prices for what they sold. Indeed, they began to grow quite rich. With all this luck, which they never had before, they decided the ring must be a magic one, for it was the only thing which was new in the house. All else was the same.

" 'The ring is a treasure, after all,' the wife said. 'We must be careful of it.'

"She went and fetched it out of the drawer. It was just the same old rusty ring, but now it was precious to them.

" 'I must make a box for it which we can keep locked,' the man said.

"So he made the box, and he put a lock on it. They put the ring in the box and locked it up safely.

" 'Now where shall we keep the box in this dirty hut?' the wife asked.

"Where indeed? They looked up and down and all around. Suddenly as she stared up into the rafters the wife had an idea. 'Let's hang it up in the rafters!' she said.

" 'That is a good idea,' the man said. 'What a smart woman you are!'

"So they tied the box up in the rafters and then they went on getting richer and richer. The man and his wife bought fine clothes and new furniture and they ate good food every day. The

dog and the cat of course had good food, too. Where they used to be given only a few leftover bits they now had fine meals of meat and fish and they grew fat and sleek.

"Alas and alack! The wife could not keep from boasting about the ring. She told only her best friend and made her promise not to tell. But the best friend told another friend whom she made promise not to tell, and that one told another, and finally a woman on the other side of the river heard about it and she told her husband.

"Now this husband was a thief. One night he crossed the river and crept into the house when the man and his wife were asleep. The dog, who should have been watching, had eaten an unusually large meal of beef and bone and was sound asleep. The thief climbed up on the table and into the rafters and stole the box with the ring.

"At first the man and his wife did not notice it. They had got so used to the box in the rafters and so used to their luck that now they did not look at the ring every day. But when they suddenly began to have bad luck, when their crops turned poor and their money was lost, they did look. The box was gone and in it the ring! How they wept and wailed! But it was no use. They grew poorer and poorer. They had to sell their fine clothes and all the new furniture and they had to eat miserable food again. Of course the dog and the cat did not like this at all. They too had no more meat and fish. Instead they had to go back to a few cold leftovers.

"The cat blamed the dog for not having caught the thief. 'How do you know it was a thief?' the dog asked.

" 'I saw him climb the rafters one night,' the cat said.

" 'Why didn't you wake me?' the dog asked. 'That is not my business,' the cat said, and she yawned and licked her paws. But they were both so hungry that they stopped quarreling. 'We must go and get the ring again,' the cat told the dog. 'You can swim the river for I don't like water, and I will ride on your back. Then we will find the box.'

" 'How will we open the box?' the dog asked.

" 'I will catch a mouse who can gnaw a hole in it,' the cat said.

"Both of them were so hungry for meat and fish that they decided to do their best. The cat caught a mouse and with the mouse in her mouth she climbed on the dog's back and the dog swam across the river. When they got to the thief's house they crawled in an open window. They found the box tied in the rafters and the cat told the mouse to gnaw a hole. The mouse was terrified of the cat, for the cat had said, 'I will eat you if you don't do what I say.' When the hole was gnawed it ran away quickly, and the cat put her paw in the box and took out the ring. With the ring in her mouth she climbed on the dog's back again and the dog swam all the way back across the river.

"As soon as they reached the shore the cat leaped from the dog's back and ran ahead to the house and gave the ring to the man and his wife, who were just waking up, dreading to begin the hard day ahead.

"When they saw the ring in the cat's mouth, they cried out for joy! 'Oh, look at this dear cat!' the wife said. 'She has found our ring!'

" 'What a beautiful cat!' the man replied. 'Now we shall all be rich again.'

" 'Dear cat,' the woman said, 'I'm going to give you the bit of meat I had saved for our own dinner. We can buy better now.'

"So she fed the cat the meat, and the cat ate it quickly and sat in the doorway washing her face with her paws.

"By this time the poor dog came loping in, wet and muddy and bedraggled. He saw the man and his wife petting the cat and praising her, and he felt very badly. He understood at once that the cat had said nothing about *his* part in getting the ring, not to mention what the mouse had done. She had kept all the glory for herself. He was so angry and hurt that he lifted his head and howled and whined and barked. When he did this the man and his wife were angry with him.

" 'Look at this jealous dog!' they cried.

" 'He does not care that the dear cat went out all alone and found the ring and brought it back to us. He thinks he should be given meat and be praised, too. But what has *he* to do with it?'

"So they fell upon the dog and gave him a good beating and he slunk away. As for the cat, she sat there in the sunshine in the doorway, purring loudly and licking her paws.

"From that day on the dog vowed that he would never be friends with the cat again. He would chase her whenever he saw her and he would make her life as miserable as he could. Moreover, he would tell his children and his grandchildren how mean she had been and they would chase cats, too, and make their lives miserable, as long as there were cats in the world."

"This was the story the old story teller told us that day in a village street in China.

" 'Is it a true story?' I asked him.

" 'We-ll-ll-ll,' he said slowly. 'It *is* quite true that dogs still chase cats, isn't it?'

"He passed his little basket at this moment and I put in my two pennies and the other people put in their pennies and the story teller counted the pennies and put them all in his pocket.

" 'Thank you and I think I'll go on,' he said, and the last we saw of him he was walking down the road, very gay, his straw hat on one side of his head, on his way to the next village."

The children knew that Grandmother did not like to be interrupted when she was telling a story, and so they were very quiet. Indeed, she almost seemed to change before their eyes. They imagined that she looked like the Chinese story teller herself, and that they were in China, too. Now they took a deep breath and came back to where they really were, here in their own country, sitting under the big walnut tree, with Grandmother. And of course Ricky had a question to ask, which he had saved up all the time Grandmother was talking.

"But do you believe the story is true, Grandmother?" he asked.

67

Grandmother's eyes twinkled just as the Chinese story teller's eyes had twinkled long ago, but Grandmother's eyes were blue, whereas, as everyone knows, Chinese eyes are always black.

"Well," she said. "Of course this is not China and so who knows what is true here? But I see your mother on the other side of the brook waving her handkerchief at you. It's lunchtime and you must be hungry. Anyway, *I* am. Good-bye, dears, and come again tomorrow! But Barky had better stay home.

"Tizzy really doesn't like dogs."

"Where shall we put the big star?" Jimpsey asked.

Jimpsey was six years old. His real name was James Collingswood Brown, but he was called Jimpsey because his mother had said one day, when she was trying to button his coat, "Oh, please stand still, Jimmy—you're such a jimpsey, jumpsey little boy!" And from that day on he was called Jimpsey.

The star was almost as tall as he was.

"Let's have a big star," his mother had said last week, "a big star to celebrate this first Christmas in our own home."

The house was one they had chosen together, a farmhouse set in meadows, and they moved there in the autumn when the trees were red and gold, and already it was home. They had lived in the city before they found the house, but Jimpsey's father said a boy should grow up in the country where there was plenty of room and that was why they were here instead of there. Now it was Christmas Eve, and Jimpsey's father had just finished the star. It was made of five crossed pieces of wood, and on each piece of wood he had fastened electric lights. They stood around it to admire it, Jimpsey, his father, his mother, and Mr. Higgins, the hired man. Mr. Higgins was old and bent over, but he had been Jimpsey's best friend ever since they had moved into the house in the country.

"Yes, it's such a big star, where shall we put it?" Jimpsey's mother asked.

"Let's think," Jimpsey's father said.

"Put it at the top of the big sycamore tree there by the front door," Mr. Higgins said. "Then the lights will shine clear down to the bridge."

"A good idea," Jimpsey's father said. "That's what we'll do."

The house stood on a hill and at the bottom of the hill was a brook and across the brook was a bridge. Jimpsey could see the bridge very easily now, as he jumped around the tree. It had three arches and it was made of stone, a pretty bridge, his mother said, and it was another reason she had wanted to buy this particular house.

Meanwhile the star was going up. First Mr. Higgins tied a rope around the middle of the star, then he fetched a ladder and set it against the tree, then he climbed up into the tree and Jimpsey's father lifted the star and Mr. Higgins pulled, until the star was high among the branches, facing the bridge.

"Beautiful," Jimpsey's mother said.

Mr. Higgins tied the star fast to a branch and then he climbed down carefully because he was quite old, and Jimpsey's father went into the house to attach the electric cord. In a moment the star was shining, and they all clapped their hands, and Jimpsey's mother sang "O Little Star of Bethlehem."

"Except this is a big star," Jimpsey said when she had finished.

"Quite right," his father said, "and now I must go about some Christmas business of my own."

"So must I," Jimpsey's mother said.

That left just Jimpsey and Mr. Higgins, and as usual they began to talk. That is, Mr. Higgins began to talk and Jimpsey listened. Mr. Higgins loved to talk, and Jimpsey liked to hear him, and so everything was all right. Mr Higgins began:

"You see the big barn, Jimpsey?"

72

"I see it," Jimpsey said.

It was easy to see, for there it stood, not far from the house, a huge old barn with a slanting roof. It was made of stone and wood, and inside the big doors were piles of hay and straw.

"You see the bridge?" Mr. Higgins asked.

"I see the bridge," Jimpsey said. He could not see it too well now, for the sun was beginning to set and a faint mist was rising from the brook. Still, he could see the three arches and the curve over the water.

"Did you know a ghost walks betwixt the barn and the bridge at midnight of every Christmas Eve?"

"A ghost?" Jimpsey repeated in a small voice.

"A ghost," Mr. Higgins said firmly. "It's the ghost of my old friend, Timothy Stillwagon, who died several years ago, come the day after Christmas."

"Why does his ghost stay in our barn?" Jimpsey asked. He was not sure that he liked the idea of a ghost, especially on Christmas Eve and in his barn.

"It wasn't your barn in those days," Mr. Higgins said. "It was the barn of Timothy Stillwagon himself. He was the farmer here and he lived in the house here and he kept his cows in the barn here, and every Christmas Eve the two of us would walk together from the barn down to the bridge at midnight, mind you, after he'd trimmed the tree for his children. I'd trim my tree for my children, too, my wife and me, and then I'd walk up to the hill to see his tree, and he'd walk back with me to see my tree, because my house is there by the bridge."

It was true that Mr. Higgins' house was there by the bridge. It was a small house, set in a small neat garden.

"Why did you walk to see your trees?" Jimpsey asked.

"Because," Mr. Higgins said, "whichever of the two of us had the finer tree, the other was supposed to buy him a cup of hot coffee at the village diner."

"Did you have the best tree, Mr. Higgins?" Jimpsey asked.

Mr. Higgins laughed in big chuckles. "Neither one nor the other of us ever got the cup of coffee, on account of we always thought each had the prettier tree. The end of that was that we'd walk back and forth betwixt the barn and the bridge arguing about it, until we could walk no more on account of the cold. And you'll be getting cold too, Jimpsey, just standing here listening to me talk about it. So go into the house before your mother calls you in."

"Good night, Mr. Higgins," Jimpsey said, "and I wish you a Merry Christmas."

"The same to you, Jimpsey," Mr. Higgins said. "And it will be a merry Christmas for me, because you are here. My own children are grown up and gone away, my old wife is dead, and I'm alone yonder in that little house of mine by the bridge, as I've been for many a year. But this Christmas, bless you, when I look up here, I won't see a dark house. I'll see a warm house with a family in it, and you the child, and above the house a big star shining. Oh, Timothy Stillwagon and I will have something to talk about at last!"

Jimpsey was surprised. "You mean you still talk to him?"

"Oh, sure," Mr. Higgins said cheerfully, "him and me, we walk the road together, just as we always did on Christmas Eve, me in my flesh and bones, and he in his ghost."

Jimpsey heard this and he was not at all sure he liked the idea of a ghost walking this very night of Christmas Eve. He went into the house and shut the door tightly and ran to find his mother. She was in the living room tying golden balls on the Christmas tree.

"Mother!" he said in a little voice. "I'm here."

She turned around, surprised. "Why, Jimpsey," she said, "you look white. Are you cold?"

"No," Jimpsey said. "It's just that Mr. Higgins says we have a ghost."

"Do we?" she said. "Well now, who is he?"

"He's a man who used to live here, Mr. Higgins says, but now he's a ghost."

His mother laughed. "Oh, that Mr. Higgins—he does talk so much!"

"Don't you believe him, Mother?"

"Not when he talks about ghosts," she said and she tied another golden ball on the tree.

At this moment, from upstairs, Jimpsey heard his father singing a Christmas carol. It was his favorite, a cheerful one, the one about decking halls with boughs of holly, and Jimpsey ran upstairs.

"Daddy," he said all out of breath. "Did you know we have a ghost?"

His father was tying a gold ribbon around a very small box wrapped in blue paper.

"Tell me about it," he said.

Jimpsey began all over again. "It's the ghost of Mr. Timothy Stillwagon. He lived in this house, him and his children."

"He and his children," his father said. "And I'm sure they had a happy life, and bless his ghost, and don't tell your mother you saw me wrapping this very small package because it's for her, and inside it is a beautiful gold bracelet made just for her."

"I won't tell," Jimpsey said and he stood watching his father tie a big bow on the small box.

"Are you afraid of ghosts, Daddy?" he said after a while.

"Well," his father said, "I've never seen one. It's silly to be afraid of something you've never seen. Fact is, Jimpsey, I don't even believe in ghosts."

"Mr. Higgins does," Jimpsey said.

"He's a lonely old man and maybe he dreams of ghosts to keep him company. And speaking of company, let's go downstairs and see if your mother needs help with the tree."

They went downstairs together and what with one thing and another, eating supper by the fire and having his bath and hanging up his stocking by the chimney piece, Jimpsey went to sleep thinking about Santa Claus instead of Timothy Stillwagon.

"Go to sleep right away," his mother said when she tucked him into bed.

"Santa Claus has a lot to do for you tonight," his father said, kissing him good night.

How long he slept Jimpsey did not know. When he woke up the house was very quiet, so quiet that he thought he would get up and see why it was quiet. He put on his slippers and his warm blue bathrobe and went to the window. The big star was still shining, so that Santa Claus could find his way, and shining so brightly that Jimpsey could almost see the bridge.

Then suddenly he saw the ghost. Slowly, slowly he saw a small figure walk out of the barn and down the road toward the bridge. He stared as hard as he could. Was it really—yes, it was really a ghost, a shadowy gray ghost in the light of the star.

For a minute Jimpsey wanted to run back to bed and pull the covers over his head. Then he remembered what his father had said. "It's silly to be afraid of something you've never seen." And instead of hiding himself in bed, Jimpsey decided then and there that he would go and look at the ghost and see whether he was to be afraid of it. It took several minutes to get into his clothes and his warm coat and his galoshes, for there was snow on the ground, but he managed. He slipped out the front door and he was glad the big star was shining across the meadow and on the road, so that he did not need a lantern from the barn. He ran as fast as he could down the road, looking for the ghost. He could not see it. He couldn't see anybody or anything, just the snowy white road lit by the star.

Now he was almost disappointed. To be so near a ghost and then lose it! He stopped running and wondered whether he should just go home and back to bed. He was not afraid—oh, no—but everything was so quiet, and beyond the edge of the light from the star was the darkness. But Jimpsey was quite a brave boy at heart and he did not give up easily and soon he began to walk again toward the bridge.

It was a good thing that he did, for now he saw the ghost again. It was sitting on the wall of the bridge and it looked very small and tired and lonely. He was suddenly not afraid any more. He began to walk briskly until he reached the bridge. Then he stopped and looked at the ghost. The light from the star was dim now, for the bridge was rather far from the house, and he could not see the ghost very well. He stepped nearer and nearer until he was quite close. Yes, there the ghost was, sitting on the stone wall of the bridge.

Now at this very minute what should happen except a big sneeze! Jimpsey had forgotten to put on his cap and the cold wind was blowing around his ears and in his hair. At the sound of the sneeze the ghost gave a start.

"Why, Jimpsey," it said, "what're you doing here at this time of night?"

The voice was not the voice of a ghost—not at all. It was the voice of Mr. Higgins. The wind blew off the ghost's hat and under it was the face of Mr. Higgins, looking very cold and wrinkled.

"I wanted to see a ghost," Jimpsey said, "and it's only you, Mr. Higgins. . . . Isn't there any ghost? You shouldn't have said there was a ghost when it's only you, Mr. Higgins."

"Well, now, Jimpsey," Mr. Higgins said. "I'm ashamed I said there was a real ghost, when it's only Timothy Stillwagon's memory that I walk with on Christmas Eve. I guess I wanted to believe he walks with me every Christmas. Of course, he can't walk in flesh and blood, the way he used to, and so I just made him into a ghost, because even his ghost would be more than nothing at all, you know. Yes, I guess it's only a memory I walk with, after all."

"What's a memory, Mr. Higgins?" Jimpsey asked.

Mr. Higgins picked up his cap and pushed it down over his ears. "It's something or somebody—you can never forget."

"Like the gray poodle dog we had," Jimpsey said. "He got sick and died when we were living in the city, but I don't forget him. His name was Buster. Is he a memory, Mr. Higgins?"

"Sure he is," Mr. Higgins said. "The same as Timothy Stillwagon. We were friends all our lives, him and me. We went fishing together when we were little boys, like you. We fished under this very bridge and caught catfish and took 'em home for supper. And we grew up and got married and had other little boys like you, and then one day it was all over and only me left—me and a memory. Timothy's not dead for me, Jimpsey. Come Christmas Eve, I walk the road from the barn to the bridge, and he walks with me as if he was alive again. Call him a ghost or not—I see him this minute, as he was alive, because we were friends. As long as you remember somebody, he's still alive—in you, if nowhere else—eh, Tim, old boy?"

Mr. Higgins turned his head and smiled, exactly as if Timothy Stillwagon were sitting there on the wall beside him.

"Do you see him?" Jimpsey asked.

"I see him," Mr. Higgins said, "but that's because I know how he looked. You can't see him, because you don't know how he looked."

"You're not afraid?" Jimpsey asked.

"Of course not," Mr. Higgins said. "Do you think I could be afraid of Timothy? I never was nor am I now. As long as I live, we're the same friends we always were."

"But when you die, Mr. Higgins?" Jimpsey asked.

"Then you'll remember me, come Christmas Eve," Mr. Higgins said, "seeing as we're getting to be such good friends already. Christmas Eve is a great time for remembering friends—not just presents, you know, but thoughts—loving thoughts."

"I'll always remember you, Mr. Higgins," Jimpsey said.

"Good," Mr. Higgins said, "I'd rather have that for Christmas than a barrel full of presents." He got up. "That wall is sitting kind of cold under me. And you ought to be in bed. I'll take you back to the house. . . . You understand what I've been talking about, Jimpsey?"

"Kind of," Jimpsey said.

"It'll come clear to you some day," Mr. Higgins said.

He took Jimpsey's hand and they walked up the hill again, in the steady light of the big star, and when they came to the house Mr. Higgins said good night and Merry Christmas again and Jimpsey said the same to him. Then Jimpsey went upstairs and put on his pajamas. Just before he jumped into bed he looked out the window and saw Mr. Higgins, very small and bent, walking down the road to the bridge.

"So now," Jimpsey told himself, "some Christmas Eve when I'm as big as Daddy, maybe I'll look out this window and see the ghost of Mr. Higgins walking down that road. Only it won't be a ghost. It'll be my memory of Mr. Higgins."

He climbed into bed and pulled up the covers. Tomorrow he would have to explain to his father and mother—explain the Christmas ghost. Tomorrow—tomorrow—and suddenly he was fast asleep.

Christmas Miniature

"The sooner you go to sleep," his little mother had told him, "the sooner Santa Claus will come. You don't want to keep him waiting, do you?"

"On such a cold night, too," his big father had said. "His toes might get frostbitten."

They had hurried him into the tub, they had scrubbed him fast and hard, laughing all the while, for he was six years old and on other nights he took his own bath. They had rubbed him with the red bath towel, red for Christmas, and buttoned him into his red pajamas, red for Christmas again. They had tossed him into his bed as soon as he had said his prayers and covered him up in his warm red quilt. When his father opened the window, the snow blew in.

"A white Christmas," his little mother cried and clapped her hands. She was still quite young, her yellow hair all curly about her face.

Sandy was her big boy. He had a room to himself while his baby sister, Dilly, slept in her crib in the nursery. Her name was really Elizabeth, but when she was born she was so pretty that her father had shouted at the sight of her:

"Oh, what a dilly!"

That was what he had shouted and her mother had laughed.

"Dilly she is," she had said, "and Dilly we'll call her."

Dilly, of course, was already asleep when Sandy was finally tucked in, kissed, chucked under the chin, and left alone to go to sleep, too.

He had gone to sleep, not at once, but after he had told himself that really he must not think about Santa Claus, who was waiting out in the snow, his toes getting frosted. He slept a long time, so long that when he woke, he thought it was late. The night before Christmas is always long, much longer than other nights, or so it seems every year. Sandy lay in his bed, wondering what time it was. The house was still, and on the floor beside the open window the snow had made a drift. Maybe he had better get up and shut the window. He pushed back the covers and crept out of bed and shut the window. Of course the right thing to do was to get back into bed, but he did want to know what time it was. He could tell time, not by minutes, but certainly by hours, and half hours and quarter hours, on the old grandfather clock in the hall at the foot of the stairs. He'd go and look at the clock and see what time it was and then run back to bed.

When he was five years old, Sandy's kind mother had given him a flashlight to use if he felt afraid in the night, which he really wasn't any more, although he had been when he was small, but she let him keep the flashlight, in case. He used it now, not because he was afraid, which he wasn't at all, but to make a round spot of light go in front of his feet like a lantern. Down the stairs the light shone steadily ahead of him. The door to the nursery was closed, and so was the door to his parents' room. Oh, how huge and quiet a house is at night! Not a sound did Sandy hear, not a footstep, not even his own, for his red pajamas covered his feet and besides there was carpet on the stairs. Down he went, step by step, following the light as though it were a star leading him. When he had taken the last step, he lifted the flashlight and let it fall upon the face of the old clock. The man in the moon, painted exactly above the XII, looked back at him, and there the hands of the clock pointed, both together. It was midnight, and the night before Christmas!

Had Santa Claus come? That was the question. The doors to the living room were closed. On Christmas, as Sandy remembered, his father shut the door into the living room so that Santa Claus could be private.

"Santa is a sort of artist," his father had said. "He likes to be left alone while he does his work. He wants to get everything just right."

Maybe it wouldn't matter if Sandy just opened the door a little crack and flashed his light through that crack, to see if Santa had come or not? For if not, then indeed he must hurry straight upstairs to bed and shut his eyes tight, so that Santa need not wait any longer. Very well, then! Sandy opened the door just enough to put the light through into the living room. There was the tree where it always stood for Christmas, between the fireplace and the picture window. Ah ha, Santa Claus had come! The tree was beautiful, shining with tinsel and bright balls, and under it—well, the heap of presents was higher than ever, although every year his father pretended to grumble.

"Good gracious, Elaine," he grumbled—Elaine was the mother —"it'll take us all day merely to tear off ribbons and paper."

And what was that gleaming so red from behind the tree? Could it be a—bicycle?

Sandy had no time to look. For suddenly he saw a horrid sight. Snips, his yellow cat, was crouched under the tree. The light glittered on his eyes and they looked like marbles of fire. But Snips was not looking at Sandy. He was looking at a very small mouse who stood helpless with fright just inside the crèche, under the tree. The mouse had run there, thinking perhaps that it was a safe place to escape the cat, who seemed, to a tiny brown mouse, as big as a jungle tiger. While Sandy stared, Snips crawled forward on his stomach to the very door of the crèche, and there he lay, enjoying the mouse before he caught her and ate her.

Sandy was horrified. He loved Snips, who was a playful cat, but

a cat is a cat, and Snips, while he had learned only to look at birds and switch his tail longingly, could never resist a mouse. Though it was Christmas Eve, he had sauntered about the house as usual, and seeing the heap of presents under the tree, he had investigated. Thus he had surprised the mouse, who had smelled cheese. There was a cheese, a nice Danish cheese, wrapped in silver paper and ribbon, for Sandy's father loved cheese, and insisted that he must be given a whole round cheese every Christmas, or he would pout all day. He always got a cheese and so no one knew whether he would pout all day or not.

It was this cheese that had tempted the mouse. She was a mother mouse, and behind the wainscoting behind the couch she had a nest of babies, each one no larger than the end of Sandy's thumb. Since she was often hungry and tired, she had left them asleep when she smelled cheese and, coming out, she had found the package and had already nibbled off a corner of silver paper when Snips smelled mouse. Cheese he disliked but mouse he loved, and so he had appeared and scared the mother mouse so that her little knees shook. The crèche was near and into the crèche she had run, taking shelter behind the tiny manger, wherein lay the tiny image of the Christ Child. Mary, the mother, knelt beside the manger, and Joseph knelt beside her.

The mouse had no time to see them. She crouched behind the manger, keeping very quiet until she thought the cat had gone away and then she stood on her hind legs and lifted her head above the manger to see if she were safe. Oh, what horror indeed! Far from being safe, she was in the greatest danger. There, preventing all hope of escape, the great cat crouched at the entrance to the crèche. He had but to put out his paw and she would be caught in his curving claws. And her babies, lying so innocently asleep, what would become of them? They would starve and die. She would never see them again.

The big cat stared at her. He, too, was thinking she could not escape. He would tease her for a while and then, when he was tired of playing, he would eat her up in a minute. Rather thin she was, a mere mouthful for a big yellow cat, but a nice mouthful. Mouse meat is delicious for a cat, very tender, the little bones easy to crunch. Snips began to purr.

In the crèche, peeping above the tiny manger, the mother mouse heard that purring. It sounded like rumbling thunder in her frightened ears. Who could hear her voice even if she squeaked? And who helps a mouse? She was quite alone. These small silent people in the crèche were hardly bigger than herself. They did not move. Perhaps they, too, were afraid of the big cat. Though it was no use—oh, no use at all—still she could not keep from squeaking. She was so afraid, so desperate.

"Please—please—please—"

That was the way her little squeaks sounded. But no one could hear her. The purring roar of the cat was much too loud.

It was at this moment that Sandy's light flashed upon the crèche and he saw what was going on.

"Snips!" he called, but not too loudly. After all, Santa might still be in the chimney.

Snips did not turn his head. He kept on purring and gazing at the mother mouse. So what could Sandy do but push open the door and squeeze through into the living room, Christmas Eve though it was? He kept his light steadily upon the crèche and just as Snips put out his paw to snatch the mother mouse, Sandy put in his hand first and caught her and saved her.

"Me—yow—yow," Snips howled.

"I don't care," Sandy said. "The idea of your catching a mouse on Christmas Eve! And right in the crèche!"

The mouse, however, did not know she was saved. She felt herself caught in a warm hand and she thought she must be in a trap of some sort. She had the kindest heart in the world, but she had never been held in a hand before, and in her fright she opened her mouth and bit the end of Sandy's thumb. It was a very small bite, not enough to hurt, for the mother mouse's teeth were scarcely bigger than the sharp end of a pin. Still, it was enough to surprise Sandy and he dropped her and she ran under the couch.

There he might have lost her except that Snips, cross because he had lost his tidbit, ran after her. Then Sandy followed Snips, and pushing the couch away from the wall, he saw the cat peering into a small hole in the wainscoting. He let the light flash into the hole, and now he knew why the mouse had been in such haste. There upon a soft nest of cotton wadding, which of course the mother mouse had pulled from inside the couch, were five baby mice, all pink, and each no bigger than the end of Sandy's thumb. And curled around them, already feeding them and cuddling them, was the mother mouse. She did not move when the bright light flashed upon her. Perhaps the light dazed her, perhaps she knew that the hole was too small for either Sandy or Snips to reach her. Perhaps she just hoped that she was safe.

"Ow—wow—wow," Snips said sadly. He knew that the hole was too small for him to get through. Even his paw was too big to reach in and bring out a mouse. There was nothing to do but wait. He crouched down and switched his tail and his jaws quivered while he watched."Ow—wow—wow," he moaned.

"Be quiet," Sandy said. He kept looking at the little family in the stolen nest. This house was not only his home, then. It was the home of another family, too, a mouse's family, mother and children, and a father mouse, who was probably out hunting for food.

"Snips, you leave them alone," he said sternly. And he stooped

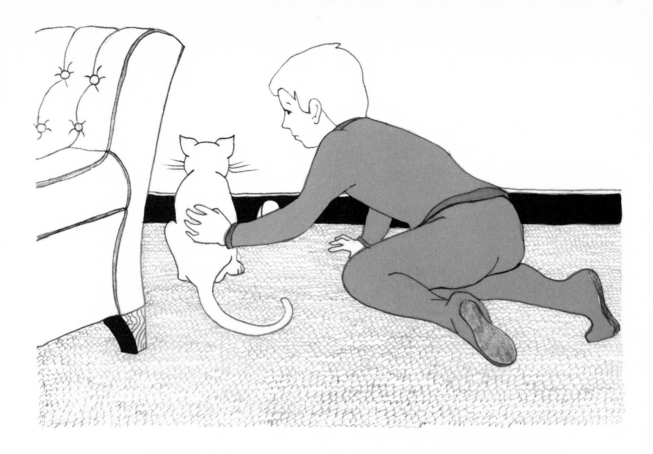

and took Snips under his arm and held him, legs and tail hanging down on one side and head on the other.

"You come upstairs with me, Snips," he said. "I'll shut the door so you can't get out again tonight."

So, with the cat hanging on his arm, Sandy pushed the couch back to its place.

He was just about to leave the room when he thought of something wonderful. Wasn't it wonderful that he had waked just at twelve o'clock on Christmas Eve, had come downstairs, not indeed to peep at the Christmas tree but only to see what time it was, and then peeping, after all, not at the Christmas tree but just to see whether Santa Claus had come and gone, and then that he had seen, quite by accident perhaps, the mother mouse hiding in the crèche? And suppose he had not come down, and suppose Snips had caught the mouse and had eaten her, leaving blood there upon the floor of the crèche, right where Mary knelt beside the little

Jesus, how sad that would have been! And what of all those mouse babies, none bigger than the end of his thumb, waiting for the mother mouse, who would then never have come back? How could it have been a merry Christmas for them? For the babies would have died, wouldn't they, and his mother would have found them sooner or later, and the sad story be told? Oh, wonderful that he had waked at Christmas midnight, and led by the light, had come to save the mouse family!

He paused by the crèche, thinking these thoughts, and the light shone in upon a peaceful scene. The hay, really only a handful of dried grass from the lawn, was piled behind the manger, and there the tiny image of Jesus slept. And Mary and Joseph knelt lovingly by, their hands folded.

Well now, he must go back to bed. He tried not to look behind the tree for it was not fair to see the presents before morning, but his light quite by accident caught the edge of something that was certainly a red wheel. He turned away firmly. No, no peeping! He tiptoed out of the living room, closing the door after him, and still guided by the light, he climbed the stairs and went to his room and shut the door. Only now did he put down Snips, the cat, who was getting heavy. Then he got into bed.

"Naughty Snips," he said, looking down at his yellow cat, who was plainly planning to get into bed with him.

Snips laid back his ears and switched his tail. Naughty?

"Me—yow—yow," he protested.

"Well—ell," Sandy said, yielding, "come along then. I suppose you don't know any better."

He pulled up the covers and tucked the red quilt around Snips, too. A cat is a cat, and Snips couldn't help being interested in mice.

"All the same," Sandy said, "I'm glad the light happened to flash into the crèche just at that minute."

And he went to sleep without any trouble at all. Santa Claus had come and gone. The baby mice were safe with their mother. And in the crèche the holy family waited for Christmas morning.

The Chinese Children Next Door

The four children were watching the sun go down behind the hill. They were all ready for bed. Peter wore yellow pajamas because he liked yellow, Michael wore green pajamas because he liked green, David wore blue pajamas because he liked blue, and Judy wore pink ones because she had brown hair. They stood at the window at the top of the stairs and the sun went slowly down until all they could see of it was a bright orange edge to the hill.

"Now where does the sun go?" David asked.

"It goes to China," Mother said.

"What is China?" Peter asked.

"China is a place," Mother said, "and it is a big place, even bigger than the whole of America where we live, and there are even more people there than here."

"How do you know?" Michael asked. He always wanted to know how people knew things.

"Because," Mother said, "when I was a little girl no bigger than five, like David and Judy, and no bigger than six, like Michael and Peter, I lived in China in a house on a hill like ours . . . except that it was a Chinese hill."

When the four children heard their mother say this, they were so astonished that their eyes and mouths flew open.

"I thought that you had always lived here in our house," Judy said. Her blue eyes were round, she was so astonished.

"No," Mother said. "When I was a little girl I lived very far from this house and this hill."

"Tell us—

"Tell us—

"Tell us—

"Tell us all about when you were a little girl," the four children said one after the other and all together.

"What!" Mother exclaimed, "when the sun has gone down and it is only half an hour to bedtime?"

"Well," David said, coaxing, "tell us just one story about it."

"Very well," Mother said, "I will tell you just one story of when I was a little girl in China."

So all the children went into Mother's room, and they sat down on the rug in front of the fire, and Mother sat down, too, and that was the way this story began.

"When I was a little girl in China," Mother said, "it didn't seem strange to me that I was in China instead of here in America like you. I used to watch the sun go down out of my window, too, and I would ask my mother, 'Where is the sun going?' And she said, 'It is going over to America. Half the time the sun shines on our side of the world and half the time it shines on the other side, and while it is our turn we play and while it is the other side's turn we sleep, and that is what makes night and day.'"

"Are the Chinese children playing now?" Peter asked.

"They are just about getting up," Mother said. "Soon they will see the light from the sun coming up over their hills, and they will begin to think about breakfast and play.

"When you are asleep in your beds, they will be running outside. That's the way I did when I was a little girl in China. I played when the American children slept and I slept while they played."

"But whom did you play with?" Michael asked. He couldn't imagine his mother so far away.

"I played with the Chinese children next door," Mother said. "They had a big family of little girls. Some were my age and some were older and some were younger, and I was just in the middle."

"Didn't they have any boys?" David asked.

"That is the story," Mother said, "and I will tell it to you. I think there is just time before you go to bed."

She looked at the clock as she spoke and there the clock was on the mantel piece, ticking away.

The hand was very near to half-past seven and half-past seven was the time that the four children were supposed to be in bed.

"Oh, how fast that clock ticks!" Judy cried. "And when we look, it goes faster."

"I'll turn it around so we can't see how fast it goes," Mother said. So she jumped up and turned the clock around and all that they could see was . . . the back of the clock with two little brass knobs on it.

"Now for the story," Mother said. And she sat down again with the children around her.

"You must know, children," Mother said, "that all fathers and mothers like to have both boys and girls in their families if they can, but in China it is very important indeed.

"The Chinese family who lived next door to us when I was a little girl were very sad because they had no boys. They liked their girls, and their girls were very nice. They all had black hair which their mother combed every day with a wooden comb, and she made it into pigtails, one to each girl, and tied the ends with bright red woolen yarn. And . . ."

"What were the girls' names?" Judy asked.

"You must know, children," Mother said, "that the Chinese don't have just the same names we do, and they don't speak our language though they say just the same things in their own language. Well, the first girl's name was Bao-bei, which means Precious. She

95

was the oldest and she was eight years old and she took care of the others. She washed their faces and buttoned their clothes and picked them up when they fell down, and did all the things that the oldest sister should do. . . . The girls all had red cheeks and bright black eyes and they laughed a great deal and were healthy and happy and hardly ever sick. But still, there wasn't a boy . . . .

"The second girl's name was En-bao, which means More Precious. She was seven years old and she helped her sister take care of the others, but she couldn't get much done because she laughed all the time—she simply could not help it. Sometimes her mother said, 'More Precious, stop laughing—it sounds silly to laugh all the time.' But More Precious would only cover her face with her hands and laugh all the more. Then I would pull her hands away and ask her, 'More Precious, what are you laughing at?' And she would laugh again and say, 'Everything!' That was the way More Precious was—she thought everything was funny.

"The third girl's name was Swen-bao, which means Plenty of Precious, and she was six years old. By that time, you can see, the Chinese mother was getting tired of not having even one boy, and she named the third girl baby Plenty.

"Before the fourth one was born everybody hoped that the fourth baby would be a boy. But no, the fourth one was another girl, a nice fat girl with red cheeks. But when she was born the Chinese mother was tired of the whole thing and she said, 'Let's stop calling all these girls Precious—let's begin with something else.'

" 'Don't talk like that,' the Chinese father said. 'People will think you don't like girls. We ought to be glad to have such nice girls with red cheeks and black eyes and pigtails. Besides, this fourth one is quite a pretty little thing.'

" 'You name her, then,' the Chinese mother said, who was still disgusted. 'I can't go on thinking up names for girls.'

" 'I shall call her Mei-Yi,' the Chinese father said, 'and that means Pretty-one.'

" 'Let's hope we don't have a Pretty-two and a Pretty-three,' the

96

Chinese mother said, who had a boy's name all picked out and now could not use it."

"What did she want to call the boy she didn't have?" Michael asked.

"She was going to call him Yung-er," Mother said, "and that means Brave Boy. But it was no use. She simply had to put the name away and hope that some day she would have a boy.

"Well, the four little Chinese girls themselves didn't mind at all that they were not boys. They played all day and ate their rice—"

"Rice?" David asked.

"Oh," Mother said, "I forgot, we ate rice in China."

"Every day?" Peter asked. He didn't like rice very much.

"Every meal," Mother said. "We had a sort of rice porridge for breakfast, with salt fish and dried vegetables and a kind of cheese made of beans that we called bean curd, and we had dry rice for the other two meals, with meat and fish and vegetables, and it was all good and I liked it. I used to eat very often with the three Precious ones and with Pretty-one. We used to see who could empty our bowls first with our chopsticks—"

"Chopsticks?" David asked.

"Oh," Mother said, "I forgot—we used chopsticks instead of knives and forks. Chopsticks are two pieces of round wood, longer than pencils and not so thick, and you hold them in your right hand and your bowl in your left and it is much easier than a knife and fork."

"How funny!" the children cried.

"If you think it was a funny way to eat," Mother said, "why, we didn't think so. What we thought was funny was eating with a knife and a fork. I remember Precious said, 'How funny that the Americans eat with a knife and a fork. Don't they stick themselves, and don't they cut their mouths?' And More Precious laughed and laughed."

"Did they think we are funny?" the four children asked one after the other. "Did they?" "Really?" "How funny!" And they all laughed because they thought it was funny that children in China think children in America are funny.

"People always think what's different is funny," Mother said. "Well, we played—"

"What did you play?" Peter asked.

"Oh, we played at flying kites," Mother said, "and we played with paper lanterns made in the shape of rabbits and fish and butterflies and flowers—"

"Lanterns?" Judy asked.

"We lit them at night," Mother said, "and they had little red candles inside and they were on wheels if they were animals and we pulled them by strings, or they were on sticks if they were birds and fish and flowers, and we carried the sticks.

"Well, we played house, too, and because the Chinese family did so want a little boy, we always played that our babies were boys. And before the fifth baby was born to the Chinese family, everybody was hoping that it would be a boy, because four girls were enough for any family anywhere.

"The Chinese mother said, 'Really I must do something about this,' and so she went to the big temple in the city, which was the same as a church is to us here, and she prayed for a baby boy and prayed very hard, indeed.

"I wish I could tell you that she did have a baby boy, and that she could have used the name she had all ready—but what do you think?"

Mother stopped and looked at Peter, Michael, David, and Judy.

"What—what—what—what?" they all asked.

"She had another little baby girl," Mother said, laughing, "a little baby girl with black hair and black eyes!"

"Do all Chinese have black hair and black eyes?" Judy asked.

"They do," Mother said, "for that's the way people look in China. Well, now there were five little baby girls, and when the mother saw this new little one, she just turned over in bed and put her face to the wall and wouldn't speak."

"Didn't she like her little baby?" Judy asked.

"Of course she did," Mother said, "but still she wanted a little boy, just for a change and just for once. Besides, there was the name, Brave Boy, all ready and waiting.

"Well, the Chinese father came in, and he was a tall gentleman with black mustache and black eyes and a kind face, and he wore a long robe of silk—"

"A robe?" David asked.

"That is what Chinese gentlemen wear," Mother said, "and they look very nice, too. And when the Chinese father saw the Chinese mother with her face turned to the wall, he said, 'Aren't you ashamed not to speak to your dear little new baby!'

"He bent over the baby's little bamboo bed and he said, 'Why, she's a very pretty little thing. I shall call her Mei-er.' Mei-er means Pretty-two. And he chucked the baby under the chin and went out again, and sat outdoors in the court and smoked his water pipe—"

"Water pipe?" Peter asked.

"That's what Chinese like to smoke," Mother said. "It is a brass pipe with tobacco on one side and water on the other, and the smoke has to go through the water, and that cools it so it doesn't burn your tongue. Well, the Chinese father sat smoking his water pipe out in the court and we were playing there. We had been playing, kicking our shuttlecocks—"

"Kicking them?" Michael asked.

"That is what we did in China," Mother said. "We took some small cash, which were copper coins about as big as our quarters over here, except they had holes in the middle. We sewed them together tightly in a bit of rag and stuck three small feathers into the hole, and sewed them in tightly, too. Then the game was to see how many times you could hop on one foot and with the other foot doubled up inward, kick the shuttlecock on your ankle and keep it in the air. . . .

"Plenty Precious could do it the best, because she was little and light . . . and Precious could do it the next best because she was only a little fat . . . but More Precious could not do it at all, because she was so fat and besides she was the one who laughed all the time.

"As for me, some days I could do it and some days I couldn't. Well, as I said, we had been playing shuttlecock in the court and waiting to hear if the baby boy had come. When the Chinese father

100

came out we all shouted, 'Is it a boy this time?'

"He looked at us, pretending he didn't understand.

" 'Who?' he asked.

" 'The new baby,' we answered.

" 'Oh, that one,' he said, 'no, it is a nice little girl, a very pretty little girl, and her name is Pretty-two.'

"We all sat perfectly still and for once More Precious didn't laugh for one minute. We all knew how the Chinese mother had wanted a boy this time, and she was such a nice mother, so kind and good and pretty, and she so often bought us sesame candy and barley toffee, that we felt sad. Then More Precious began to laugh again.

" 'How can you laugh?' her sister Precious asked her crossly.

" 'Oh, it's so funny,' More Precious giggled, 'It's so funny that all our boys are girls!'

"Well, then, we all laughed and we went on kicking the shuttlecocks and we forgot about babies until the next year when it was time for another one. By that time Pretty-two was the cutest, fattest, funniest little baby you ever saw, and her father loved her better and better every day, so that wherever he went, even when he went outside the gate and down the street to the tea shop—"

"Tea shop?" David asked.

"That is where Chinese gentlemen all go to talk with other Chinese gentlemen and drink tea and eat their favorite foods and have some peace and quiet away from their families and too many children," Mother said laughing. "Well, when the Chinese father went to the tea shop he couldn't bear to leave Pretty-two behind and so he always told a young servant girl to bring her along and he walked in front, his long silk robes swinging and his water pipe in his hand, and behind him would come the girl carrying Pretty-two . . . who was the fattest, cutest, funniest baby, all dressed up in red silk coat and trousers, with a little Buddha cap on—"

"Buddha cap?" Judy asked.

"A Buddha cap," Mother explained, "is the kind of cap lots of the Chinese babies wear. It hasn't any top and it is like a crown and in front are sewn eight little tiny gold Buddhas. Through the top Pretty-two's little tight pigtail stood right up, tied with red yarn.

"Everybody thought it was strange for the Chinese father to take Pretty-two to the tea shop, but he didn't care. He said Pretty-two was so funny that he digested his food better if she were with him, and soon Pretty-two became a great favorite with all the gentlemen in the tea shop and they would watch her and laugh and laugh . . . while she smiled and sucked her fingers and bubbled at them."

"Do the Chinese babies do such baby things, too?" asked Judy who likes babies very much.

"Chinese babies do exactly the same things our babies do over here," Mother said, "and they are just as cute with their red cheeks and black eyes and little black pigtails tied with red yarn. And when the Chinese father saw how all his friends enjoyed Pretty-two he grew very proud. He set her on the table among the tea bowls and he put on his spectacles and he cleared his throat and he made little speeches. He said, 'Girls are just as good as boys, and I like my five girls just the same as I would like the five boys I haven't got, and I shall treat my daughters exactly the same as the sons I don't have.'

"At this Pretty-two would smile, though not understanding it, and look so cute that he would have to . . . stop and smell her cheeks—"

"Smell her cheeks?" Peter cried astonished.

"That is the way fathers and mothers kiss their children in China," Mother said, "and they say lovingly 'Ping-hsiang,' and that means, 'How very sweet'—"

The four children laughed at this, but Mother simply shook her head. "I can remember," she said, "how funny the Preciouses used to think it was when my American mother kissed me! 'What is she doing?' Plenty Precious asked me one day. 'Is she going to bite you?' And More Precious laughed until she had the hiccups. So you see, we are funny, too.

"Well, to go back to Pretty-two, that was the way the Chinese father felt about his girls. But the Chinese mother still wanted a boy. She grew quite angry about it and she would argue and say, 'If other mothers can have a boy why can't I have a boy?' And she thought about going out and finding a baby boy who had no father and mother and bringing him home and making him her little boy. But she decided she would try just once more. If perhaps by some chance—"

The four children leaned forward on their elbows and breathed hard. "Was it a boy baby?" Judy whispered.

Mother looked from one face to the other. "Do you know," she said solemnly, "it was another girl, and when the Chinese mother saw another little round face with black eyes and black hair and red cheeks she burst out crying as loudly as she could.

"The Chinese father was in his study writing a letter with a brush—"

"With a brush?" David asked surprised.

"Chinese do write with brushes," Mother said, "just like your paint brush, and the ink is like a piece of black paint in your water color box. They dip it in water and rub it on a stone dish. Well, when the Chinese father heard the Chinese mother crying he dropped his brush and hurried into her room as fast as he could in his velvet shoes—"

"Velvet shoes?" Peter asked.

"That's what gentlemen wear on their feet in China," Mother said, "and the Chinese father said to the Chinese mother, 'Mother of all my girls, why do you cry?'

"She pointed at the bamboo cradle which by now was pretty well used, and she said, 'Look in there!'

"He looked in and he saw the new little girl and he burst out laughing as he took her up in his arms. She was very small and he said, 'I've been expecting you,' and he laughed and he laughed, and he smelled her tiny red cheeks and said she was the prettiest baby yet. 'Why, my little Pretty-three,' he said, 'Ping-hsiang, ping-hsiang!' and then he put her back in her cradle and said to the Chinese mother, 'You are a wonderful woman. Each girl you have is prettier than the last and no man could ask for a better wife.' And then he went back to his study and finished his letter."

"Didn't they ever have a boy?" Peter asked.

"That is the end of my story," Mother said. "At first the Chinese mother said, 'Don't talk to me about any more babies. I have done my best, and what is it?—six girls!'

" 'Well, I give up.' But the Chinese father said, 'Don't give up so easily, mother of my girls.'

"So after three years the Chinese mother decided that maybe she had given up too easily and she decided that she would try just one more baby. Of course this time, she said, she knew she would simply have another girl, and she would not go to the temple, and she wouldn't get any new clothes ready. She said the new baby could just wear the clothes left over from all the other girls—she didn't care."

"Was it another girl?" Judy asked.

All the four children leaned on Mother's knee with their elbows digging in and listened with their mouths opened. And Mother laughed and laughed.

"We all expected a girl," she said. "I remember we were playing together, the three Preciouses and the three Pretties and I, and we didn't even stop playing when the nurse came out of the Chinese mother's room.

" 'How is the new baby girl?' I called while I was playing. 'Oh,' the nurse gasped, 'Oh—quick—Precious, More Precious, Plenty Precious, and Pretty One, Two, Three—go and call your father— it's a *Boy!*'

"Well, how we did run to look for the Chinese father! But we couldn't find him anywhere. He wasn't in the study, writing with his brush and he wasn't in the tea shop drinking tea though the gardener ran there to find him. Do you know where he was?"

"Where?" the children breathed.

"The gardener ran all over the streets looking for him," Mother said, "and at last he . . . found him in the bath house taking a bath."

"The bath house?" Peter asked.

"Chinese gentlemen don't bathe at home," Mother said, "they go to a bath house and buy a bath. Well, the Chinese father was sitting in a stone bathtub full of very hot water, having his back scrubbed by a bath boy, when the gardener bawled through the half-open door, 'The new baby has come, sir!'

"The Chinese father was enjoying his bath very much, and he called back lazily, 'I'll be home soon. Meanwhile, call her Pretty-four.'

" 'Sir,' the gardener shouted, 'it's a *Boy!*'

"Well, the gardener said afterwards, you should have seen the Chinese father! He leaped out of the tub and threw on his clothes,

105

and . . . went home so fast that everybody thought the house was on fire except that he looked too cheerful for a man whose house was burning up and . . . he rushed through the gate and tore across the court and into the Chinese mother's room.

"The Chinese mother was sitting up in bed with her best red satin jacket on and her hair freshly brushed. She had put a red pomegranate flower into her knot and looked perfectly beautiful.

" 'Greetings, father of my son,' she said proudly when the Chinese father came in.

" 'I don't believe it,' he said.

" 'There he is,' she said, pointing at the old bamboo cradle. 'Of course we must get a new cradle at once,' she went on, 'and it is a disgrace that we have only the girl's old clothes to put on him!'

"The Chinese father went over to the cradle and . . . stood looking down at the baby boy.

"He was a nice baby, but the Chinese father felt queer having

a boy. He was not prepared for it, being by now so used to girls. 'He is not as pretty as the girls,' he said at last.

"This made the Chinese mother cross. 'Of all the ungrateful men!' she cried, and her black eyes sparkled with anger.

" 'Don't be cross with me, mother of my girls,' the Chinese father said. 'After all, I am not used to this sort of—of baby.'

" 'Brave Boy is a very fine child,' the Chinese mother said.

" 'Doubtless he is,' the Chinese father said but doubtfully. Then he said to the Chinese mother, though still astonished, 'Well, if you are satisfied, I must be, I suppose.'

" 'You had better be,' the Chinese mother said."

Mother stopped to laugh again, as she thought of the Chinese father and mother.

"Was that the end of the babies?" Judy asked.

"The very end," Mother said. "There never was another baby in that house. The Chinese mother said she had only wanted to make sure she could have a boy and there was no use in going on and on after she knew she could."

"Was he a nice boy?" David asked. "When he got bigger, I mean?"

"Brave Boy?" Mother asked. "Oh, he was a very nice boy. We played with him all the time and took care of him and dressed him up and fed him and he was just like a doll. We all loved him, and especially his six sisters loved him.

"Of course he didn't have a pigtail tied with red yarn, because boys have their hair cut off in China, too, and he wore little robes like his father and velvet shoes. But the Chinese father always said the girls were the nicest because they were so pretty, much prettier than Brave Boy was.

"But then he didn't need to be pretty, being a *Boy.*"

Mother got up and turned the clock around as she spoke.

"Heavens!" she cried, "The children in China will have had their breakfast ages ago! It's high time you were in bed and sound asleep!"

The
Water-Buffalo
Children

"Did you have to speak Chinese?" Michael asked Mother. His eyes grew round.

"Certainly I did," Mother said. "When I was a little girl I lived in China where all the children speak Chinese."

"Do they mind?" Peter asked.

"Certainly not," Mother said. "They think it is the way to talk, just as you think your way is the way to talk. They feel very sorry for you, having to speak English."

The four children were sitting at the dinner table and the reason they were talking about China was that their mother had surprised them.

It was Saturday. They had played outdoors all morning doing only the things they liked to do. Just when they were thinking what to do next and just when David had said, "I am getting hungry," the big bell that hung on the porch began to clang.

Clangety-clang-clangety-clang! They knew when that big bell rang it meant "come home right away." So they hurried as fast as they could. There was Mother on the porch, and there was Daddy, smoking his pipe.

"There's a surprise!" Daddy called.

In exactly three minutes and a half, for Daddy timed them with his watch, they were washed and ready.

"Shut your eyes," Daddy said.

So they shut their eyes.

"Hold hands," Mother said.

Daddy took Peter's hand, for Peter is the oldest, and Mother took Judy's hand, for Judy is the youngest, and Michael and David were the betweens. They all marched to the dining room.

"Open your eyes!" Daddy said.

So they all opened their eyes and saw—the surprise. It was on the table. It was a Chinese dinner!

"How queer!" Judy said.

"It isn't really queer," Daddy said. "It's very good."

In the middle of the table were five bowls of food, all steaming hot, and at each place was a bowl of flaky dry rice, steaming hot.

"Everybody has rice at a Chinese dinner," Mother said.

"There are no knives and forks," David said.

"There are chopsticks," Mother said.

So that was the surprise, and everybody sat down, and they all learned how to hold their chopsticks in one hand and their bowls in the other.

At first they were not sure they liked all the new tastes. But after one bite and two and three, they decided they did like them, and it was fun to eat with chopsticks. Then Mother began to tell them the Chinese names of all the dishes, and then Michael asked how Mother knew those names and then she said, "Because when I was a little girl I lived in China and played with Chinese children and talked Chinese."

"Which Chinese children did you like best?" Judy asked.

Mother had to think hard to answer that. "Well," she said at last, "next to the Chinese Children Next Door, I think I liked best the Water-Buffalo Children. They were brother and sister."

At this the children put down their chopsticks, since they were really very full.

"Tell us about the Water-Buffalo Boy," Michael said.

"No, tell us about his sister," Judy said.

"I'd rather hear about the Water-Buffalo," said Peter, who likes animals.

"What *is* a Water-Buffalo?" David asked.

"I'll tell you about all of them," Mother said. "But perhaps I had better begin with the Water-Buffalo, because I saw her first."

So she began with the Water-Buffalo.

"You must know, children," she said, "that the Water-Buffalo is a very strange beast. She looks like a cow because she is shaped like a very big cow, but she isn't a cow."

"Why not?" asked David.

"Because her horns are too wide and long," Mother said, "much wider and longer than a cow's horns. That's the first reason. She hasn't a skin like a cow, either, but much more like a rhinoceros, thick and black and without much hair, and that's the second reason she isn't a cow. And she is called a Water-Buffalo because she likes to get right under the water like a hippopotamus, and that's the third reason she isn't like a cow. And I suppose there is a fourth reason, and it is that, though she can give a little milk if she has to, she isn't used for milk but to pull plows for farmers."

"Plows!" Peter cried. Peter knows all about farming things because he likes farming. "Why, that's funny!"

"If you lived in China you wouldn't think it was funny," Mother said, "because almost everybody plows with Water-Buffalos there. Now this Water-Buffalo was called Big Turnip—"

The children burst out laughing. "Turnip!" they cried—"Big Turnip!"

"Because she was so very slow," Mother said. "It is not strange for a Water-Buffalo to be slow for they are all slow. They would all rather stand still than walk and they would rather soak themselves under water than anything else. But Big Turnip was the slowest of all slow Water-Buffaloes. The farmer to whom she belonged was Mr. Ching. He called her Big Turnip because she was so slow that she made him angry, and Big Turnip—well, it's what you call things in China that make you angry."

"Like dumb-bell," Peter said quickly.

"Exactly," Mother said. "Only of course the sound of Big Turnip was not that—in Chinese it is Da Lobo. So the Water-Buffalo was called Da Lobo, for Da is big and Lobo is turnip.

"Now I can remember very well the very first day I ever saw Da Lobo. I had done my lessons early and my mother was a very busy woman and so I ran outside the gate with my story book and some peanuts so I wouldn't be under her feet, and I made a nest for myself in the high pampas grass outside the gate. The grass was so high that it was over my head, and I tramped down a nice round spot and when I sat down I could see out but nobody could see me. Then I opened the story book. It was 'Arabian Nights,' I remember, because I had just got to the story of Aladdin's lamp, and I cracked my peanuts, and I was having a beautiful time. The sun shone down into my little nest so warmly, I remember, and the crushed grass had a sweet smell under me, and far away in the valley a thrush sang a loud clear song. There was no wind, and it was a day in spring, not too hot and not too cold, and I remember feeling perfectly happy."

"I know that kind of a day," Judy said. "We have them here too."

"We do," Mother said. "Well, it was that kind of a day. I felt very good inside, I remember, for I had done my lessons well that morning, and I had all the afternoon just for myself. So I kept on reading and eating peanuts and I came to the place where Aladdin rubbed his lamp, and I read on and he found the princess and I read on to the end of the story when they all lived happily ever after. When I finished the story I didn't feel like starting another right away. I lay on my back looking into the sky and thinking, 'What if I had a magic lamp?' I sat up and looked around me in the pampas grass. What if I found an old rusty magic lamp? Sometimes I did find strange things on the Chinese hills. There were old graves on them, made long ago, which people had forgotten, and the wind blew on them and the rains soaked them and sometimes the sides wore away, and I found old jars and bowls in them that the long ago people had put there as we put flowers now. These jars I dug

out and washed and kept in what I called my museum. Well, I
looked around me that day in the pampas grass, but I didn't see
anything strange except a small very pretty white polished stone.
It was an unusual stone to find there, where the land had few
stones anyway. I picked it up and thought, 'What if this is a magic
stone?' I held it a while and the longer I held it, the more I felt
perhaps it was a magic stone. So when I began to feel quite sure,
I rubbed it as Aladdin rubbed the lamp—you remember?"

"And what happened?" David whispered.

"Nothing, the first time," Mother said. "So I held it a little while
more to warm it up, and then I said 'Abracadabra!' just for good
measure and I rubbed the stone hard, and then—"

Mother looked around at their faces. Even Daddy had taken his
pipe out of his mouth and was listening.

"Something did happen," Mother said. "The tall pampas grass
began to move, and I stooped and looked through the green stalks
and I saw legs and four black hooves and a thin swishing tail, and

I began to be a little scared. But what could I do except to sit still and wait? In a minute the legs were near, and the four hoofs came close, and I looked up and there above me was the big head, with wide black horns, of a Water-Buffalo! She had a big ring in her black nose, and there was a rope in the ring and it was wound around her neck. I jumped up, really afraid now, at what had come out of the stone, and I shrank back from the big face, and the big black eyes as big as tennis balls, and the great horns.

" 'Oh, dear,' I cried, 'I wish I hadn't!'

"Then I saw what I hadn't seen before. On the back of the big Water-Buffalo were two children, one a boy about my age, and I was eight, and a little girl not bigger than five. They stared at me, and I stared at them, and pretty soon I saw they were as afraid of me as I was afraid of the Water-Buffalo and so I wasn't afraid any more. At last the boy felt brave enough to speak first.

" 'Are you the foreign girl that lives in the house on top of the hill?' he asked me.

"Why did he call you foreign?" Michael asked.

"Because I was foreign to him," Mother said. "He was a Chinese boy in China, and he had black hair and black eyes, as all the Chinese have, and I was an American child living in China, and I had blue eyes and yellow hair, which he thought very funny.

"So I said, 'Who are you?'

" 'I am Big Brother,' he said, 'and this is Little Sister, and the Buffalo is Da Lobo.'

"I laughed, just as you did, at the idea of calling a Water-Buffalo Big Turnip, and so I said, 'Why is the Water-Buffalo's name Da Lobo?'

" 'Because she is so slow she makes my father angry,' Big Brother said.

"All this time Little Sister had been holding him tight around his bare waist with her clasped arms, and she had not said one word.

"But she was a very pretty little girl. She had a round face and a small red mouth which she kept open all the time so you could see her teeth that were as white as rice, and her black hair was braided in one braid with a piece of scarlet yarn threaded through the braid, and she wore straight black bangs almost down to her round black eyes. Both she and Big Brother were barefoot, and Da Lobo's back was so wide that their legs stuck straight out.

"Da Lobo, seeing that we had begun to talk, took the chance to stand still and do nothing, as she always did if she could. She rolled her eyes around to see what there was to eat, and chewed on the nearest pampas grass, although it was so tough and its edges so sharp that nothing but a Water-Buffalo could have eaten it.

" 'Come down,' I said to the two children. 'Let's play.'

"So Big Brother slid down, and when he slid Little Sister slid, too, for she did not let go of him for one minute, and when they both reached the ground she stood with her arms still tightly around his waist and peeping at me over his shoulder.

" 'Why is she afraid of me?' I asked Big Brother.

" 'How should I know?' Big Brother said. 'She's only a girl.'

" 'I am a girl, too,' I said, 'and I am not afraid. At least I was only afraid for a minute of Da Lobo because I thought she had come out of my magic lamp—I mean my magic stone.'

" 'Where is your magic stone?' Big Brother asked.

"I picked up the white stone then. I had thrown it down when I was frightened of Da Lobo, and I held it out in my hand for him to see.

" 'Is it really a magic stone?' Big Brother asked, staring at it hard.

" 'When I rubbed it Da Lobo came with you on her back,' I said.

" 'But we were coming anyway,' Big Brother said. 'We were on our way to the other side of the hill to graze there. Father finished the rice plowing this morning and so he told me to take Da Lobo out to grass this afternoon, and to take her somewhere to find good new grass, so that was why we came this way.'

" 'Maybe the stone isn't magic,' I said.

" 'You rub it,' Big Brother said.

" 'No, you rub it,' I said.

"We were both a little afraid to rub it.

" 'You ought to rub it,' I said at last, 'because you're a boy.'

"Of course then Big Brother had to show that he was brave and he stepped forward and Little Sister clinging to his waist stepped forward too and when he found her still there he grew cross with her.

" 'Let go, you little rabbit,' he said, and pulled her arms off his waist so that she began to cry.

118

" 'Don't call her a rabbit,' I said, for you must know that in China you don't call people rabbits because it is not nice, and when I saw poor Little Sister standing there with her big eyes full of tears, I felt so sorry I went and put my arms around her.

" 'You are *not* a rabbit,' I said, 'and he *is* a turtle.'

"This was naughty of me, for in China it is just as bad to call people turtles as it is to call them rabbits.

" 'I am not a turtle,' Big Brother said.

" 'Then Little Sister is not a rabbit,' I said.

"He thought about this a minute, but he really was anxious to try the stone, and so he said,

" 'Let's not talk about rabbits and turtles,' and he picked up the stone, and rubbed it a very little. Nothing happened.

" 'You have to say "Abracadabra," ' I said.

" 'What is that?' he asked astonished.

" 'It's a magic word,' I said.

" 'If it's foreign magic, I won't say it,' he said.

" 'It's not foreign magic, it's just magic,' I told him. 'See, I will write it for you,' and I took a stick and smoothed a place on the hard ground and scratched the word on it as plainly as I could.

" 'I can't read,' he said, 'I never went to school. But those letters don't look right to me. I never saw any like them. They must be foreign letters. I would rather not say it.'

" 'Then the stone won't do its magic for you.' I told him.

"He thought a while about this and then he said, 'I'll take the stone home and keep it overnight and if I dare to say it tomorrow I'll come back here when the sun is half way between the hill and the top of the sky,' and he pointed his finger to the spot.

" 'What if you still don't dare?' I asked.

" 'Then I'll come back and tell you so,' he said, 'and I'll give you back the stone.'

"So he put the stone inside his girdle, for he only wore short pants and his girdle was a strip of blue cloth wrapped around his waist and he used it for pockets as well as to keep his pants up.

Then he shouted at Da Lobo who all this time had been standing very still, chewing the grass and not liking it very well as you could see from the tired look in her eyes, but still she kept on chewing it instead of moving along to anything better, because she was very lazy. But when Big Brother shouted she obeyed him like a lamb, although she was a huge beast and he only a small boy.

" 'Down!' he shouted.

"At the sound of his voice she put down her head and he leaped on it, holding himself by her great horns, and he crawled up her neck and in a minute, a second, much quicker than I can tell you about it, he was on her back again with his legs sticking straight out. Then Little Sister took hold of Da Lobo's stringy tail and climbed up her back legs just as briskly and sat herself behind him with her legs sticking straight out.

" 'Until we meet,' they both said, which is the way you say good-bye in Chinese.

" 'Until we meet tomorrow,' I said.

"Da Lobo knew of course that now she must move but she didn't until the very last minute she had to, and that minute was when Little Sister turned round and twisted her tail hard. Then Da Lobo blew air through her big nose, and very slowly she moved her big body and soon all I could see were the two dark heads of Big Brother and Little Sister above the tall pampas grass."

Here Mother stopped to remember and to smile, because she forgot where she was. Whenever Mother did this the children wanted her to come back to them quickly out of what she was remembering, which was so far away.

"Mother, Mother!" Judy cried.

Peter slipped out of his chair and came running around the table to lean against Mother.

"Don't stop, Mother," Michael said.

"Was it a magic stone?" David asked.

"How did I know?" Mother said. "I couldn't decide, myself, even when I went home I didn't tell anybody, because if you tell about magic things they aren't magic any more. In the night, when I woke up and heard the big bell in the temple boom through the darkness, I thought about the stone and it seemed to me then that it must be magic. But I was always a little afraid of the sound of the bell in the night. That bell had thunder in it. I had been in the temple and stood near it when a priest struck it and the sound was louder than thunder. At night, alone in my bed, I could feel it rolling up the hill like thunder."

"I'm afraid of thunder," Peter said in such a small voice that Mother gave him a squeeze.

"I used to be afraid of thunder, too," she said, "and maybe that is why the big bell always scared me a little. So that night when I heard it I was sure the stone was magic. But when I got up in the morning and ate a big dish of porridge just as I always did, and saw the sun shining everywhere around, I wasn't so sure about the magic.

"I hurried through my lessons that day, I remember, though I had three times three to learn and usually I was slow at multiplication tables. My mother was so surprised that she asked me what I was going to do after my lessons and she hoped it wasn't anything naughty that made me so quick.

" 'Oh no, it's not naughty,' I said, 'It's only something magic but I can't tell you about it until afterward.'

"So when the sun was exactly half way between the hill and the top of the sky and exactly at the spot where Big Brother's finger had pointed yesterday, I was in my nest in the pampas grass waiting. I didn't have to wait long. In a very few minutes I saw the two heads bobbing over the top of the tall grass, and in a minute more the grass parted and there was Da Lobo again, looking exactly as she had yesterday, but today I wasn't afraid of her. And there, too, on her back, was Big Brother in his short blue cotton pants. I could see the stone bulging in his girdle, and behind him was Little Sister in her little faded red jacket and blue pants, and she was clutching him around the waist, and their bare legs were sticking out. But Big Brother looked very solemn.

"'Big Brother and Little Sister,' I said, 'have you eaten your rice?'"

"Why did you ask that?" David asked Mother.

"Because," Mother said, "that is the polite way in China to say, 'How do you do?'

"Big Brother was polite, too.

"'I have eaten,' he said. 'Have you?'

"'I have,' I said.

"Little Sister was not so shy today, and at this moment she piped up. 'But you don't eat rice,' she said. 'You are a foreigner and you eat rats and dogs and cow's fat.'

"'I do not,' I said. 'Whoever told you such lies?'

"'That's what we've always heard about foreigners,' Big Brother said.

"'I eat just what you eat,' I said. 'I eat rice and meat and vegetables.'

"'But you do eat cow's milk and cow's fat,' Little Sister said.

"'It's not cow's fat—it's butter,' I said, 'and it is good, especially on bread.'

"'I wouldn't eat it,' Little Sister said. 'I'd be afraid it would make me smell.'

"'If you go on talking like that,' I said to Little Sister, 'I shall be sorry I wouldn't let Big Brother call you a rabbit yesterday.'

"At this Little Sister shut her red mouth and stared at me very hard, and Big Brother turned around and pretended to slap her.

"'You have no manners,' he said to her. 'What will this foreign girl think of you?'

"'That's all right,' I said, trying to be nice. 'She's very small.'

"'Yes, she is,' Big Brother said, 'and besides she is only a girl.'

"'But I told you I am a girl,' I cried when he said this again.

"'You mustn't mind me,' Big Brother said quickly. 'I have no manners either. Besides, you don't look like a girl. You are so big.'

"Now I saw he was trying to be nice and so we all forgave each other, and Da Lobo stood perfectly still as she always did when she had a chance and chewed pampas grass with a tired look because she didn't like it any better today than she had yesterday.

" 'This stone,' Big Brother said, taking the white stone out of his girdle, 'is a magic stone. I have decided that.'

" 'Why do you think it is?' I asked.

" 'Because,' he said, 'it is so white that in the night it could be seen on the table near my bed. And my father saw it when he came in and he said, "What is that so white on the table?" and I said, "It is a stone," and he lit the candle and took the stone in his hand and he said, "It is a strange stone. I never saw such a smooth white stone. Don't lose it." Even he thought it was strange so it must be magic.'

" 'Then do you want to say "Abracadabra" today?' I asked him.

" 'I will rub the stone,' he said, 'and you say that word.'

"So that was what we did. I said 'Abracadabra' three times very slowly and he rubbed the stone, while Little Sister held on tight and shut her eyes."

"What happened?" Michael whispered.

"Nothing," Mother said, "nothing at all, though we all waited. A bee flew out of the grass, a big yellow and black bumble bee, but that was nothing. A little green snake slithered out and saw us and slithered away again, but that was nothing. Little Sister opened her eyes at last and all the time Da Lobo had not stopped chewing.

" 'It doesn't work that way,' I told Big Brother when we had waited a long time. 'The same person has to rub and say "Abracadabra" or the genie won't come.'

" 'Then you do it,' he said, holding out the stone to me.

" 'If I do you won't get your wish,' I said.

" 'I'll tell you what I want,' he said quickly. 'I want—'

" 'No, don't tell me,' I cried out. 'If you tell your wish you won't get it.'

"Now we were in a predicament.

" 'Predicament' is a long hard word, as a predicament is hard to get out of.

"What could we do? At last Big Brother set his teeth and screwed up his round brown face.

" 'I'll say it,' he said, holding the stone in both hands. 'I'll say it and rub at the same time.'

"Then he thought of something. 'What if Da Lobo is frightened and runs when the genie comes?'

" 'Da Lobo can't run,' I said laughing.

" 'Yes, she can,' Little Sister piped out. 'The first time she saw a white man she ran four miles into the next province.'

" 'Yes, she did,' Big Brother said. 'She can run very fast when she's scared.'

"Here was another predicament.

"What would we do if Da Lobo did run? She would run away with Big Brother and Little Sister and leave me standing there with the genie and no wish ready.

" 'I don't want to be left here all alone,' I said.

" 'You get on Da Lobo, too,' Big Brother said quickly. 'There is plenty of room. My older brother used to sit on her with us before he got married. You can sit between us so you won't fall off.'

"It seemed a good idea. He slid down over Da Lobo's head, and held her by the ring in her nose while I tried to climb up. But Da Lobo didn't like the idea of my sitting on her at all."

"Why not?" Judy asked.

"She was used to her own kind of children but not to me," Mother said. "She tried to hold her head up high so I couldn't get on her, and she rolled her eyes around and spat out the pampas grass she was chewing.

"Big Brother beat her with his fists and called her a few names and then he wound the rope around his foot so she had to keep her head down and I climbed up and sat in the middle of her back and Little Sister put her arms around me.

" 'You do smell of milk,' she said sniffing, 'and you do smell of cow's fat!' "

124

"I turned around and sniffed her. 'And you smell of garlic,' I said, 'garlic and pig's fat.'

" 'Do I?' she said. 'But that's what I had for dinner!'

"While we were talking Big Brother was unwinding the rope and tying it again around Da Lobo's neck where it usually was, and in a second he had climbed up her back and was in front of me, and I was clutching him around the waist. Da Lobo's back looked so broad, but it was really very slippery, and her backbone was sharp and it was hard to sit right on top of it. Besides, it was the very first time I had ever sat on top of a Water-Buffalo. It looks easier than it is."

Mother was laughing again and now so was Daddy.

"I can just see you," Daddy said, laughing. They both looked at each other laughing and as though they had forgotten where they were, remembering.

"But was the stone magic?" Peter asked, to bring them back again to here and now.

125

"Well," Mother said, "I will let you decide. For this is what happened. When we were all settled except Da Lobo—"

"What was the matter with Da Lobo?" Peter asked.

"She kept turning her long neck to stare at me," Mother said. "It seemed to me I saw a queer look in her big black eyes. She looked as though she were counting us. It seemed to me she was saying to herself, 'Is it one—two up there, or is it one—two—three?'

" 'I don't think Da Lobo likes me to be here,' I told Big Brother.

" 'It is because you do smell of milk,' Little Sister said, 'and it makes her feel uncomfortable.'

"Da Lobo turned her big head up this way and looked at me and she turned it up that way and looked at me, and each time she turned, one of her horns stuck into my thigh a little because her horns were very long and being in the middle I was just in the right place to be poked by them when she turned her head.

"Big Brother reached down for the rope and unwound it again.

" 'Da Lobo,' he shouted, 'your mother and grandmother were accursed!' And as he said this he pulled the rope so hard that Da Lobo shivered her skin and we nearly all slipped off.

" 'She does that when she doesn't want us on her back,' Little Sister said.

" 'Let's hurry up and try the magic stone and then if nothing happens I'll get off,' I said. So Big Brother took the stone and rubbed it and repeated after me 'Abracadabra.' "

"What happened?" Michael whispered.

"Well," Mother said, "nothing, because you see he couldn't say it just right. He said 'Ablacadabla,' because 'r' was hard for Chinese to say. I had to repeat it again and again, and I showed him how my tongue went against my teeth to make 'r,' and all the time Da Lobo was heaving her big round sides in and out so that we felt we were sitting on a folding thing like an accordion. Then suddenly Big Brother said it exactly right, and he rubbed the stone at the same time and—"

Mother paused and looked at the listening children. All the eyes were fixed on her face, even Daddy's.

"What did happen?" Judy whispered.

"Something happened," Mother said. "For the moment he shouted 'Abracadabra' just right and rubbed the stone, Da Lobo gave a great squeaky bellow and threw up her head and ran. How she ran! She ran through the pampas grass down the hill, over the rough places and over the smooth, and we clung to each other, and Little Sister shrieked and cried, and Big Brother pulled on the rope and shouted and cursed and we all hung on to each other and it was exactly like riding an earthquake. We bounced in the air and from side to side, and we dug in our heels and clung together, and barely didn't fall off. As for Da Lobo, nothing could stop her. She heaved and panted and ran, her head down, and the ring pulling her nose so that it must have hurt dreadfully. But she didn't care. She ran straight for the place she loved best and felt the safest in, and where do you suppose that was?"

Nobody could imagine and so nobody answered.

"It was in the big pond at the bottom of the hill," Mother said. "We saw her heading for it but we didn't dare to fall off because she was going so fast. We just held each other and shut our eyes and the next minute we were all in the pond, and the muddy water was around our necks. We were still sitting on Da Lobo. We could feel her big quivering body under us, but all we could see of her was the black pad of her nose above the water, breathing in and out in big snorts.

"Of course everybody came running from the paddy fields to help us, and Big Brother's father was the first to get there, and he waded in and picked us off, one by one. He was a very nice man, and he didn't scold at all. Instead when he had set us on the bank he asked,

" 'What under the sky made Da Lobo run? I never saw her run like that before.'

" 'It was the magic stone,' Big Brother faltered.

" 'What magic stone?' Mr. Ching asked. He was a farmer and he

127

wore his work clothes, which were a pair of blue cotton pants, rolled around his bare knees, and his clean brown back was bare except for a strip of blue cloth he used to wipe his sweat away when he was hot. Now we had made him quite wet and so he wiped himself while he talked.

" 'That stone you saw on my table last night,' Big Brother said.

" 'Where is it?' Mr. Ching asked.

"Where was it? We looked at each other. 'I had it in my hand,' Big Brother said, 'when Da Lobo carried us all into the water.'

"He held out both his hands. They were empty.

" 'You must have dropped it,' said Mr. Ching. 'In that case it is lost in the mud at the bottom of the pond.'

"We looked at each other sadly. Now how would we ever know whether that stone was magic or not?

" 'Da Lobo must have seen something,' Big Brother said. 'Because she never runs when she doesn't see anything.'

" 'Unless she is stung by a bee,' Mr. Ching said, looking at Da Lobo. She was still under water except her black nose.

" 'There was a bee,' I said doubtfully.

" 'Or it may have been a snake,' Mr. Ching said. 'Da Lobo hates snakes. I know when she feels one in the mud when we are plowing for rice she shakes all over and tries to lift her four feet at once.'

" 'There was a snake,' I said.

" 'Maybe she didn't like you,' Little Sister said cruelly to me. 'After all, you are a foreign girl and you do smell of milk.'

" 'Pei!' Mr. Ching cried quickly to her. 'How rude you are, Little Sister!' He sniffed me a little. 'You smell a little different from us, but it's a nice smell,' he said to make me feel better.

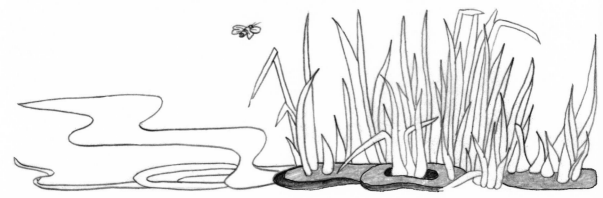

"By now he had wiped himself dry. 'Now,' he said, 'you had better all go home and change your clothes.' Then he turned to the pond. 'Da Lobo!' he cried. 'Come out!' But Da Lobo would not come out. Her black nose only snorted.

"He picked up a bamboo stick that lay near by, for they kept it there to prod Da Lobo with when she did not want to come out of the pond and go to work, and he felt under the water and gave her two or three good digs. At this Da Lobo's head came up for one minute and she looked around. Then she went down again so deep that not even her nose showed. There were only a few bubbles.

"Mr. Ching gave up. 'Well, well,' he said, 'let her drown!' He didn't mean this because he knew Water-Buffaloes have to come up. They can't stay under water too long. But he said it loudly to show her he did not care, and he went home, and Big Brother and Little Sister went after him dripping, and I dripped my way up the hill. Every now and then I turned to see whether Da Lobo was still under water, and by the time I was at the top of the hill she was out and eating grass on the bank, and I saw Mr. Ching sneak up on her and grab the end of the rope and march her home again. Then I went in to change my clothes and tell my mother what had happened to me."

"What did she say?" Peter asked. He was interested because he is himself the kind of boy who is always falling in the water so that over and over again Mother had said, "Really, Peter, I don't know what to do with you."

"What did my mother say?" Mother repeated. "Why, when she saw me standing there all dripping, she said, 'Really, child, I don't know what to do with you!' "

They all laughed at this and Daddy got up and lit his pipe.

"Good story," he said. "Wasn't it?" he asked the children.

None of them answered for a moment. It was Michael who spoke first. "But, Mother," he said, "was it a magic stone?"

Mother threw up her two hands. "How can I ever know?" she said. "Nobody knew except Da Lobo, and she couldn't tell!"

The
Beech Tree

One day when Mary Lou came home from school she found her father doing something new. He had put a big piece of white paper on the kitchen table and he was drawing lines on it with a ruler and a black pencil. Mary Lou had skipped into the kitchen to get an apple and that was how she happened to find her father there.

"Where's Mother?" she asked first of all.

"She is getting Timmie up from his nap," her father said.

Timmie was Mary Lou's baby brother.

"What are you doing?" she asked next, but after she had taken a bite of apple.

Her father looked important. He pursed up his lips as though he were going to whistle. Then he said, "I am going to build something."

"A playhouse?" Mary Lou asked. She was always wanting a playhouse, and since her father was a carpenter, it would be easy for him to make one for her.

"That comes next," her father said.

"Then what *are* you doing?" she asked again. Sometimes her father made her impatient because he was a tease.

133

"I am going to build a room on to our house," her father said.

"For me?" she asked.

Her father looked at her and made a funny face. "Can't you think of somebody else?" he asked.

"But who else?" Mary Lou asked. "Oh, Daddy, please tell me! Don't just be funny."

"Well," her father said, "your grandfather is coming to live with us."

This was such news that Mary Lou took three bites of apple before she asked another question. "You mean my grandfather from Kansas?"

"The same," her father said. He leaned over the paper and drew a line very carefully.

"Why is he coming to live with us?" Mary Lou asked.

"Well, he is getting old and he needs us," her father said.

"It's a long way, isn't it?" Mary Lou asked.

It was such a long way that she had never even seen her grandfather, because she lived in Pennsylvania.

"Is he coming on the train?" Mary Lou asked.

"He is," her father said, "and we will all go to meet him."

"When?" Mary Lou asked.

"When your summer vacation begins," her father said.

"That," Mary Lou said, "is two whole months away."

"All right," her father said, "then in two months."

She leaned over the paper on the table, where her father had drawn a big square and a little square. She put her finger on one and then the other.

"Bedroom," her father said, "and bathroom. Nice, isn't it?"

"Why can't he sleep in the room with Timmie?" Mary Lou asked.

"He needs a room to himself," her father said, "and so does Timmie."

Mary Lou felt that she had to think things over and so she skipped away to find her mother who was still upstairs with Timmie because he had just waked up and wanted to be held. Her

134

mother was sitting in the rocking chair holding him and rocking back and forth. But she looked sober instead of smiling.

"Oh, there you are," she said when she saw Mary Lou. "I was just wondering where you were."

"I was downstairs talking to Daddy," Mary Lou said. "Mother, are you glad that Grandfather is coming to live with us?"

"I hope he will be happy here," her mother said.

"Why wouldn't he be happy?" Mary Lou asked.

"Well, he's old," her mother said.

"Very old?"

"Yes, very old," her mother said.

"Fifty?" Mary Lou guessed.

"That's not old," her mother said. "At least not very old."

"Sixty?"

"Older than that," her mother said.

"Whew!" Mary Lou whistled. "Seventy?"

"And more," her mother said, "but you mustn't ask him how old he is."

"Why not?"

"Because it's not polite," her mother said.

"Why isn't it polite?" Mary Lou asked. "I like people to ask me how old I am."

"You won't when you are as old as Grandfather is now."

"But why not, Mother?" Mary Lou asked again.

Her mother suddenly got a little cross. "Oh, I don't know, Mary Lou. I wish you wouldn't keep asking questions."

Mary Lou knew that her mother was not really a cross woman, and when she was cross, it was because something had happened that she did not like and it was better not to ask her what it was. Instead it was better to try to help her until she felt better. So Mary Lou said, "I will take Timmie outside for you, Mother. It's nice and warm."

"Thank you," her mother said. "That would be a help."

Mary Lou asked no more questions for that day and she put

Timmie's coat and cap on, which she could do very well because she was already eight years old and in the third grade, and then she took him outdoors into the yard and played in the sandpile with him until it was suppertime.

At suppertime she still felt she had better not ask questions because her mother was not smiling yet and her father was quiet, and this was because he knew, too, that the mother was a little cross. It was hard for Mary Lou because by this time more questions were waiting inside her head to be asked. But she had to keep them there for her father had told her not to ask questions when Mother did not smile and Daddy was quiet.

"Just keep still and do what you are supposed to," he had told her. "You may as well learn early as late, Mary Lou."

So she had learned and while she ate supper she thought instead of talked and then she decided that it did not matter very much. When Grandfather came she could ask him all the questions she wanted to, except of course how old he was. After this it was not hard to wait, and most of the time she just forgot about it.

Meanwhile the days passed, and each day it was exciting to see how much of the new room her father had made. Every evening as soon as he came home from his job he worked on the new room, and soon it began to look very nice. When the floor was done and the walls papered, Mary Lou's mother put down a green rug and at the windows she hung some green and white curtains.

"It's a nice room," Mary Lou's father said proudly.

"I hope Grandfather appreciates it," her mother said and she was not smiling again.

Now, why, Mary Lou wondered, did her mother not smile as much as she used to? She waited until her mother had gone into the kitchen for something and then she asked her father.

"Daddy, why doesn't Mother smile about Grandfather's coming to live with us?"

"She's afraid she won't be able to take good enough care of him," her father said.

"But I'll help her, the way I do with Timmie," Mary Lou said.

"Good girl," her father told her. "You do that and everything will be all right."

This made her so happy that she could not keep from telling her mother that night when she was being tucked into bed.

"Mother," she said, "I am going to help you take care of Grandfather when he comes here to live."

But still her mother did not smile.

"You had better wait and see how he likes children," she said.

Mary Lou was surprised. "Why wouldn't he like children?" she asked.

"Sometimes old people don't," her mother said.

"Why don't—" Mary Lou began.

Her mother did not let her finish. "Go to sleep," she said. "It's late."

So there was another question not answered.

"Oh well," Mary Lou told herself, "when Grandfather comes I'll ask him that one, too. He'll tell me."

When Grandfather finally came there were quite a lot of questions that Mary Lou had saved up, but of course she could not ask them all at once. She had to wait until she knew him. They went to the station to meet him, her father and mother, Timmie and Mary Lou herself. They stood on the platform and soon the train came rushing in and stopped with a bang. Doors opened, steps were let down and people began pouring out.

"How will we know which old man is Grandfather?" Mary Lou asked her father.

"I'll know him," he said, trying to look at every door at once. Suddenly Mary Lou saw him run toward the back of the train. An old gentleman, very tall and thin, with white hair and a white beard and brown eyes, was getting down from the train. He carried a cane to help him. Mary Lou heard her father shout loudly.

"Father, here we are!"

It made her feel queer for a moment to hear her father call

somebody else "Father." She felt mixed-up. Suddenly for the first time she understood that her father had once been a little boy. She knew it, of course, for he had told her stories about living in Kansas, where he had sometimes been quite a mischievous boy, but it had always seemed to be another boy he was talking about. Now she knew it was really he, because here was his own father, this old, old man.

"Well, Son," Grandfather said in a quiet sort of voice. "It's nice to see you." He stood leaning on his cane while they all came to shake hands with him. "And this is Mary Lou and this is Timmie."

Grandfather was speaking their names in a kind low voice. Then he turned to their mother and smiled. "Marian, my dear, it's very good of you to let an old man share your home."

"You're welcome, I'm sure, Father," she said.

"Daddy," Mary Lou said, "I want to whisper to you."

"Excuse us," her father said. He leaned over and Mary Lou whispered in his ear. "Is Grandfather tired?"

"He's had a long train trip," her father whispered back.

They walked along the platform together then, and they got in the car and drove home, and Grandfather did not say anything more. He looked ahead from the front seat and Mary Lou and Timmie sat on the back seat with their mother. At last they were home and Mary Lou's father got out of the car first and helped Grandfather to get out of the car and he took Grandfather's suitcase and carried it to the new room. They all went to the new room

138

with Grandfather to see how he liked it.

"It's not quite finished," Mary Lou's father said. "I want to put in some bookcases."

"I hope you like the rug," her mother said.

"It's very nice," Grandfather said. "Very nice, indeed. I thank you all."

"Then why don't you smile?" Mary Lou asked.

"Mary Lou!" her mother cried, "you shouldn't ask such questions."

"That's all right," Grandfather said. "Children have to ask questions because it's the way they learn. I'll be smiling in a day or so, Mary Lou. Just give me time."

"We'd better let Grandfather rest," Mary Lou's mother said, and she took the children away with her and Grandfather shut the door.

"Why does he shut the door?" Mary Lou asked.

"Old people like to be quiet," her mother said.

"All the time?" Mary Lou asked. She was quite astonished because the one thing she did not like was to be quiet. It made her feel lonesome.

"I'm afraid so," her mother said. "But no more questions! You'd better help me set the table."

There was something very different about the house now that Grandfather had come to live with the family. Mary Lou felt happier than she had ever been before, but she did not know exactly why. Sometimes Grandfather was quite a lot of trouble. He had aches and pains in his bones and then he could not walk very well and there were even days when he had to stay in bed and Mary Lou's mother had to take his meals into his room on a tray. This made her too busy and then she was a little cross again.

"Mother," Mary Lou asked her mother one morning when they were having breakfast together, and Grandfather could not get up, "do you wish that Grandfather hadn't come to live with us?"

"Mercy no," her mother said. "It's just that I am too busy."

"We'll all help you more," Mary Lou's father said.

"Then I needn't be cross," her mother said and smiled quite nicely.

"Let me take the tray to Grandfather," Mary Lou said, getting up.

"Here it is," her mother said, "and thank you very much."

Mary Lou took the tray carefully and carried it to the door of Grandfather's room and then she called.

"May I come in, Grandfather?"

"You may," he called back.

She went in and there he sat up in his bed, looking very nice and clean, his face washed and his hair brushed and even his beard brushed.

"Here is your breakfast, Grandfather," Mary Lou said. She put the tray on the little table by his bed.

"Thank you, my dear," he said. "I wish I could use my legs instead of yours but this morning they decided not to work."

"Why?" Mary Lou asked. One nice thing about having Grandfather in the house was that he always had time to talk. There ought to be one grownup in every house who has plenty of time to talk and especially to answer questions.

"Well, my legs have walked me around for a very long time," Grandfather said. "I suppose we can't blame them if they feel tired now. They do their best."

"How do you know when they are tired?" Mary Lou asked. "They can't talk, can they?"

"They send their messages up to my brain," Grandfather said. "The brain is the boss. And the legs use the nerves, which are little threads like telephone wires, and they let the brain know how they feel today."

"How do they feel?" Mary Lou asked.

"They sent up word that they ache," Grandfather said. "They feel weak at the knees. Then my brain lets me know that I had better not walk on them for a day or so."

"Will my legs ever get that way?" Mary Lou asked.

"Certainly," Grandfather said cheerfully. "But don't bother about it now. Just you run and have a good time."

There were other days when Grandfather's legs felt better and then he liked to walk with Mary Lou. On such days he joked. He said, "I really have three legs, for I think I should count my cane, don't you?"

Mary Lou laughed. "But that is a wooden leg, Grandfather!"

"All the better," Grandfather said. "It doesn't get tired."

"It might break, though," Mary Lou said.

"Then I could get a new one," Grandfather said, and his brown eyes smiled.

"It is too bad," Mary Lou said one day when they were walking, "that we can't buy new real legs for you, Grandfather."

"But we can't," Grandfather replied. "That's one thing we all have to remember. We are given a nice new body to start out with when we are born, and we must keep it clean and healthy for we shan't get a new one—not in this life."

"Is there another life, Grandfather?" Mary Lou asked.

"We hope and believe there is," Grandfather said.

Mary Lou felt warm and happy when she talked with Grandfather. He always seemed quiet and happy and that made her quiet and happy, too, especially since they never had to hurry. Even walking with Grandfather was quiet and happy. If she felt like running she ran ahead and then came dancing back to him. She did it now.

"I do like to see you run," Grandfather said. "It's a pretty sight."

Mary Lou thought of something. "Does it make you feel sorry that you can't run, Grandfather?"

"Oh no," Grandfather said. "I have run many miles in my time. When I was your age I ran everywhere I went. I was always in a hurry. I had my turn at running. This is your turn. And when you're old like me, it will be other children's turn."

Mary Lou stopped. Here was something she had never thought of before.

"Will I be old like you, Grandfather?"

"I hope so," Grandfather said. "For if you don't live to be old it means that you die young, and that's a pity."

"But, Grandfather!" Mary Lou cried.

It suddenly seemed frightening to think that she must one day be old and walk slowly and stay in bed whole days because her legs ached. Oh, and her pretty brown hair would grow white, and her smooth skin be wrinkled like Grandfather's!

"You won't mind," Grandfather said. "It will be natural. The years slip along just as day and night slip along now, and you hardly notice it, do you?"

"No," Mary Lou said in a solemn voice.

While they walked they had come to the edge of a field and there was a big beech tree. Mary Lou knew it very well because in summer when there was no school the children on her street would play in the shade of the big beech. It was a very old tree, more than two hundred years old, her father said, and the top was dying.

"Look at the old beech," Grandfather said, pointing at it with his cane. "What do you see, Mary Lou?"

143

"Just an old, old tree, Grandfather," she said.

"Is that all?" he asked.

She looked again. "That's all I see except some little switches of trees growing around it."

"It's those little trees I see," Grandfather said. "Do you know where they come from, Mary Lou?"

"Just wild, Grandfather?"

"No," he said. "They come from the beech. That old tree knows that its time is about over and so what does it do? It tells its tired roots to send up a lot of little new trees. The new trees drink in the earth-water at first from the old tree's roots, and then they start roots of their own. By the time the old tree dies, they don't need it any more. They have their own life. Still, if it hadn't been for the old tree, they wouldn't be alive. So the old tree keeps on living in them."

"You mean you are like the old tree, Grandfather?"

"I am, Mary Lou," he said.

"And Daddy is the new tree—and Mother?"

"And you and Timmie," he said. "It's the way life goes. You see how it never stops."

They stood for a moment looking at the great old beech, and Mary Lou remembered a question she had forgotten to ask.

"Grandfather, you love children, don't you?"

"I do," he said. "I love them very much."

"I can feel it," Mary Lou said and she put her hand into his.

Then Grandfather said, "That's enough for one day, Mary Lou. We've been thinking big thoughts, and sometimes big thoughts are heavy. If you keep thinking about them, though, they get lighter because you understand them better. The better you understand anything the easier it is."

They walked home again and when they got there Grandfather went to his room to rest and Mary Lou skipped out to play. She was not tired at all. She felt happy because it was interesting to talk to Grandfather. She was beginning to love him very much, too.

Imagine then how she felt when that same night after supper

she heard a strange conversation between her mother and father!
She was up in her room getting ready for bed. Timmie was already
asleep and so was Grandfather. He always went to bed right after
supper, the way Timmie did. But it was a beautiful warm night
and Mary Lou found it hard to go to bed, and after her bath she
leaned out of her window. It was just above the porch and on the
porch her father and mother were sitting and talking. Mary Lou

did not mean to listen, but she could not help hearing what her mother suddenly said.

"Donald"—that was her father's name. "I really think we should consider putting your father into a nursing home. He is getting so feeble."

Her father did not answer for a while. Then he said in a queer voice, "Whatever you say, Marian. I know the burden falls on you."

"It's not that," her mother said. "It's that I don't think it's good for the children to have an old person live in the house so long. It will make them sad. Besides, I have to tell them to be quiet in the mornings when he's asleep, and maybe when he is sick they will have to keep quiet all day, and that is hard on them. After all, it is their home, not his."

Her father said in the same queer voice, "Whatever you say, Marian."

This was what Mary Lou heard and for a minute she could not believe it. Send Grandfather away just when she was beginning to love him? And he was so interesting. Oh no! She crept into bed and lay on her back, her arms under her head, and she could not sleep. Who would have time to talk with her and answer her questions if Grandfather went away? Who would have told her about the beech tree, for example? Why, Grandfather was hers and Timmie's, and how could Daddy and Mother send him away? Tears came into her eyes. Maybe it was because Grandfather spilled things and Mother had to wash more shirts and table mats. The other day Grandfather had even upset his coffee on the dining-room rug. Once when he had breakfast in bed he upset his whole tray and the sheets had to be changed. Maybe Mother was tired.

"Then I'll take care of him," Mary Lou thought. "I'll tell him to hide his clothes if he spills on them, and when I come home from school I'll wash them in his bathroom."

She could not go to sleep for thinking, and when at last she did sleep it was not for long. Her trouble woke her up in the middle of the night. Everybody was in bed now and the house was still.

She could not hear a sound except that far away an owl hooted. She got up and went to the window. The moonlight was shining, not brightly for the moon was low, an old moon her father said, and it was slipping down behind the hills, beyond the field where the great beech stood. She thought of the beech and how its branches leaned over the new little trees.

Suddenly a light shone out of a window downstairs. It was in Grandfather's room. Then he was awake, too. It would be a good time to tell him that she was going to wash his things. They would have to keep it secret, of course. She tiptoed down the stairs and knocked softly on his door.

"Come in," Grandfather said.

She went in and shut the door behind her. He was leaning against his pillows reading a book.

"Grandfather," she said, "we must talk softly so nobody can hear us. We have to keep it a secret. I am going to wash your clothes now if you spill anything on them."

Grandfather looked astonished. "What are you talking about, Mary Lou?"

She had to tell him then what she had heard her mother say on the porch. "It isn't that Mother doesn't want you here," she said. "It's just that she is too busy and she thinks you would be more comfortable in the nursing home."

"I see," Grandfather said in a low voice.

"But I don't want you to go," Mary Lou said. She was quite surprised to find that suddenly she had to cry and she began to sob. "I like you to live here, Grandfather—it makes me feel better—"

"Thank you, dear," Grandfather said in the same low voice. "And it is very sweet of you to want to wash my things, Mary Lou. But I think maybe your mother is right. I may live a long time yet, you see, and some day you would find it troublesome, too, to wash my things and that would make me feel badly. Don't cry, dear."

"But the little trees like to stay with the old beech," she sobbed. "They don't send it away."

147

"Hush, my child," he said. "Trees are not human beings."

She was kneeling by the bed now so that she could see him better and he stroked her hair. "It's time for you to be asleep," he said.

"Aren't you going to sleep, Grandfather?" she asked, wiping her eyes on the sheet.

"Old people don't need to sleep so long," he said. "Goodnight, Mary Lou, and don't you worry about me. Wherever I am you can come and see me."

"You shan't go," she said. "I won't let you."

"Thank you, dear child, for wanting me to stay," Grandfather said. "And goodnight again."

She felt better after she had cried and told him her trouble, and she went back to bed and slept.

The next day when she came home from school her father was bringing Grandfather's trunk down from the attic. Mary Lou stopped where she was, just inside the door, and dropped her books on the floor.

"Grandfather is not going," she said in a loud voice.

"How did you know, Mary Lou?" her father asked, much surprised.

"I say he shan't go," she said and stamped her foot.

Her mother heard the noise and came out of the kitchen.

"But Grandfather wants to go," she said. "This morning after you went to school he told us that he would be happier if he went to a good nursing home, not too far away so that you could come and see him."

"No," Mary Lou said, beginning to cry. "No, no, no!"

"Why, Mary Lou," her mother said.

"The child is upset," her father said. "Come here, Mary Lou, and tell me what's the matter."

Her father sat down on the bottom step of the stair and she sat down and cried on his shoulder.

"Now then," her father said, patting her back, "what's it all about?"

Mary Lou could not help telling him everything.

"I heard you," she said. "I heard you talking last night. It's not true about Timmie and me being sad. I like Grandfather to be here. He is so interesting. And he isn't busy all the time. And he explained about the big beech, and the little trees."

"What is the child talking about?" her mother said. "What has it to do with the big beech?"

"You come with me," Mary Lou said, crying very hard, indeed, "come and see the big beech and I'll tell you what Grandfather explained—"

There was nothing for it except to go with her. Timmie was playing in Grandfather's room where it was quiet and he could make a house with his blocks that he kept under Grandfather's bed, and Mary Lou and her father and mother went down the road to the field where the big beech stood, sheltering the little ones.

"There it is," Mary Lou said. "Grandfather is just like that beech. He's old, too, but he's ours. We're the new trees, don't you see, growing out of his roots."

"Roots?" her mother said, not understanding.

"Oh Mother," Mary Lou said impatiently. "I know Grandfather isn't really a tree, but he's something like it. Can't you feel how Grandfather is like the old beech? And how you and Daddy and Timmie and I are the new trees? You have to feel it—I can, can't you?"

"I can," her father said gently. "I feel exactly what you mean, Mary Lou."

But her mother said nothing. Perhaps she still didn't feel.

"Those little trees will grow old some day, too—Grandfather said they would," Mary Lou went on. "There will be other new trees then."

Still her mother said nothing. Maybe she was beginning to feel.

"Mother," Mary Lou said, "would you like it if some day Timmie and I sent you away? When you are old?"

"No," her mother said thoughtfully, "no, I wouldn't like that."

"Oh, Mother," Mary Lou said, "now you know how to feel about Grandfather! Please don't let's send him away. I'll wash his things, I'll sweep his room. But I want to keep him because he's ours."

"Well," her mother said. "This is all very strange."

"There is a good deal in what Mary Lou is trying to tell us, Marian," her father said.

"If that's the way she feels," her mother said, "then I take back what I said last night."

"Thank you, my dear," he said. "We'll all be happier, I think."

So that was the way it ended. They

walked home together and as soon as they got there Mary Lou's father took the trunk upstairs again. Then they went into Grandfather's room. Timmie was putting a steeple on a church he had built while they were away and Grandfather was sitting in the rocking chair watching him. On the bed were some neat piles of clothes he had got ready to put in the trunk.

"You may as well put those clothes away again, Father," Mary Lou's father said. "We have decided that we can't spare you. You'll just have to stay with us."

Grandfather looked up surprised. "But I thought—" he began.

"No buts, Grandfather," Mary Lou's mother said in a nice bright voice. "Mary Lou took us down to the big beech tree and explained how she felt."

"Oh, Grandfather," Mary Lou said, "please, please, stay with us!"

Grandfather's cheeks were suddenly very pink above his white beard. "Well," he said, "well, well, well—if that's the way you feel—"

"Oh, I do," Mary Lou said.

"Then so do I," Grandfather said.

And he stayed and they were all happy ever after.